"If you need ~~~~ ck, I'll ~~~~ d

"No, ~~~~ r on you, anyw~~~~

"It's v~~~~ ded, sliding her fingers up and down the flannel fabric. "It feels…good."

He let out a deep hot breath. This sexy stranger seemed to be sending him an invitation, but he couldn't be sure. He desperately tried to hold on to his last thread of control. Then he saw the tops of her breasts peeking out of the shirt. The thread snapped. He groaned and did what he'd been aching to do all night. He kissed her.

Silently, hungrily she responded with a passion that scared him. She kept her eyes open as he slid his hands beneath the shirt. He started for a moment when he realized he was touching her bare skin—and nothing else. Then she slid her arms around his neck and melted against him, making him forget everything else. Tearing his lips away from hers for a moment, he gave her one final chance to back out. "Are you sure about this?"

She met his eyes, her gaze sure and direct. "That I want you? Absolutely. That it's smart? Not at all." She held out her hands to him. "So you better stop talking, Ranger, and make love to me before I change my mind…."

Dear Reader,

Every woman dreams of the perfect lover. As readers, we like these tortured heroes, the bad boys and the loners. Mitchell Dane, the responsible older brother, was the tortured hero in my last book, *Bedroom Eyes*. Now Mitchell's little brother, Texas Ranger Jesse James Dane, can kiss his days as a bachelor goodbye. Jesse hides behind his badge, living by rules and regulations. Or he does until Cat McCade sweeps into his life and turns it upside down.

Photographer Cat McCade has found a technique to take ordinary men and make them extraordinary on film. And sometimes she even takes them home for a one-night stand. But she never lets anyone get close to her—until she meets Jesse....

A traffic accident, a wild thunderstorm and an even wilder attraction take them both to a place they never expected to be. And that's just the beginning....

I hope you enjoy *Look, But Don't Touch*. I love to hear from my readers. You can write to me at P.O. Box 67, Smyrna, GA 30081, or e-mail me at sandrasmy@aol.com.

Enjoy,

Sandra Chastain

Books by Sandra Chastain

HARLEQUIN TEMPTATION
768—BARING IT ALL
843—BEDROOM EYES

LOOK, BUT DON'T TOUCH
Sandra Chastain

HARLEQUIN®

TORONTO • NEW YORK • LONDON
AMSTERDAM • PARIS • SYDNEY • HAMBURG
STOCKHOLM • ATHENS • TOKYO • MILAN • MADRID
PRAGUE • WARSAW • BUDAPEST • AUCKLAND

ISBN 0-373-69123-8

LOOK, BUT DON'T TOUCH

Printed in U.S.A.

1

CAT MCCADE drove her gleaming black Harley into the restaurant parking lot, gunned the motor, then let the bike glide to a stop in a no parking area. She peeled off her black helmet and shook out a waterfall of straight blond hair that fell to her shoulders. Once she'd dismounted, she removed her jacket, slung it over her shoulder, and strode toward the front door on long, leather-clad legs.

It was Friday night and Cat could feel the eyes on her as the noisy patrons of the Atlanta Tex-Mex restaurant turned to look as if a television star had entered their midst. She ignored them, searching for Bettina, who would have a table and margaritas waiting. She could always depend on Bets.

From the time Bettina had hired Cat as a photographer for the models in Bachelor in a Box, they'd been friends. She'd gone on to become very successful in supplying phantom bachelors for women without permanent mates. The client selected a photograph of her fictitious lover and a "relationship" was established wherein Bettina sent gifts, letters and placed telephone calls to make it all seem real. The only problem was, on her off hours Bettina used her matchmaking efforts to arrange *real* relationships for her family and friends. And that included Cat.

"Cat! Over here."

Waiters and patrons stood back, allowing Cat to move through the crowd to her friend who was waving at her from a table in the corner. Bettina was drinking something pink and slushy. At the other place was a mug edged in salt and filled with an icy-green liquid.

Cat sat, picked up the mug and took a sip. "Not bad, Bets."

"Best margaritas in Atlanta and you know it."

"Ah, Atlanta, our hometown. No place like it. But by Monday I'll be in San Antonio along the River Walk, drinking the south-of-the-border variety."

Bettina gave her a look of bemused disbelief. "You just got here and now you're leaving? Of course you are. You never stay anywhere long enough to unpack." She tilted her head. "You know, I often wonder what you're running from."

"Not from," Cat amended quickly. "To. There's a whole world out there, ready and waiting for me to find it."

"And what's *it*?"

That stopped Cat for a moment. "*It* is my job," she said. "I'm a photographer. I enjoyed the architectural shoots and nature studies but, quite frankly, I got tired of being an assistant, and I'm just not into bugs and wild animals. What can I say? I like the comforts of hot water and good food. And being able to sleep in my own bed at night—alone."

"So that's why you photograph men, to sleep alone? I'll admit you're a challenge to my matchmaking abilities. But I'm up to it. After all, I found my brother, Mitchell, a wife who's willing to travel with him."

"I repeat. I'm not looking."

"I know. But don't think I'm not on to you. You like to be the one to call the shots. It just seems to me that a woman like you who works with men all the time could find at least one who suits her."

One thing about Bettina Dane, she didn't give up. To her, Cat couldn't possibly be happy until she had a husband or at least a significant other. "Lots of them suit me…through a camera lens. I like my life, just like it is. And that's how I intend to keep it. I've seen too many desperate women willing to give up everything to keep a man."

"Cat. Look at your sisters. They're happy, aren't they?"

"I knew a long time ago that I wasn't like my sisters. They didn't like the location moves that came from being military brats. I did. When they married and settled down, they sent out roots that have gone so deep they hardly take a vacation. They say they're happy—" Cat shrugged "—but so does my mother."

"What makes you think she's not?"

"Because she has no life of her own. In the military, an officer's wife is simply an extension of him. And now he's retired and she's switched to caring for grandchildren. She's never had her own identity." There was a catch in her voice when she said, "That's never going to happen to me."

"I know how much you worry about her, but you're carving out a lonely life for yourself," Bettina said. "Who exactly are you waiting for?"

"I'll know him when I see him. But, for now, I like my life just fine. Besides, where's *your* significant other, girlfriend?"

Bettina sighed and admitted, "You're right. You either marry at eighteen and divorce at twenty or you suddenly realize you're thirty and there are no available men interested. But the difference in me and you is that I haven't given up. I like men. I'm just selective."

"To each her own. Your relationships are selective. My relationships are impersonal."

"That's what you told me when you did your first photographs of the hunks for my Bachelor in a Box portfolio. Your work may be impersonal to you, but I have to tell you, Cat, the poor guys who were your subjects told me that it affected them a little differently. They said you're a vamp."

Cat smiled. In a way Bettina was right. She could have used experienced models for that shoot but she preferred real men and she'd had to learn how to make them relax. "So? Any good photographer develops her own techniques and if a little flirting gives me what I want on film, I reap the results. The men feel important and nobody gets hurt. And occasionally...well, there's nothing wrong with enjoying your work so long as you move on. That much of the military life I liked."

"Being a military brat didn't seem to bother you," Bettina agreed.

"Hated the rules and regulations. Loved the travel."

Bettina took a look out the front window at Cat's bike and nodded her head in the direction of the parking lot. "I can see that. A motorcycle? I don't know why that surprises me. Do you intend to ride it to Texas?"

Cat laughed. "I wish. No, I'm driving the El Camino."

Bettina rolled her eyes. "The truck? I can't get over that. You have the looks of a sex goddess—every man you meet falls at your feet—and you drive a truck?"

"The El Camino isn't a truck. It's a sleek, restored, classic vehicle, a cross between a truck and a convertible. It may not be your style, but I love it. Tell me, what are you driving these days?"

"I drive a white Honda Civic, and the only way anybody notices it is if I park it illegally."

"Bettina, you may be supplying imaginary lovers for women who are satisfied with a picture and a few phone calls and gifts. But you have the opportunity to see these guys up close and personal. I say you ought to buy yourself a red convertible and drive out to audition your bachelors personally."

"Not interested," Bettina said. "I don't mix business and pleasure."

"You don't have *any* pleasure. My career *is* my pleasure and it works fine for me."

Bettina nodded. "I suppose. But, unlike you, I think it's important to build roots. Your sisters may have established domestic roots—well I'm building business roots. Haven't you ever stopped to think where you'll be in ten years?"

That made Cat pause for a moment. The future was always out there. She told herself she'd know it when she arrived. She sure as hell didn't have a game plan to get her there. "Someplace exciting. But for now the near future is enough for me to think about."

"So what's the new assignment?"

"I'm going to Texas to shoot a catalog for Sterling Szachon. You've heard of him, haven't you? He's

Texas's answer to Donald Trump, a love-'em-and-leave-'em tycoon who's opening a chain of underwear shops for men."

"I've heard of him," Bettina said. "Sounds dangerous. Better keep your distance and stick to scouting for those yummy models."

Cat slapped her hand down on the table. "I know. Why don't you come with me and help me look for men?"

For a moment Bettina looked startled, then studied Cat thoughtfully. "No way, but I know who might be able to help you—my brother Jesse. He lives in San Antonio."

"Jesse? Well, I always hire a local assistant. If he's looking for a job, I'll talk to him."

"Jesse, a photographer's assistant?" Bettina chuckled. "I don't think so. He's a rules-and-regulations Texas Ranger now."

"I guess that means he wouldn't consider posing for my catalog. If I said you told me to look him up to add him to my portfolio, he'd probably run the other way."

Bettina laughed. "You got that right. I don't know what I was thinking. Forget looking him up. You two would never get along anyway, you run away from rules and regulations. Beside, Texas Rangers only operate in Texas."

The conversation shifted to Bettina's new service,

Rendezvous. The idea for the service had come about after a busy executive had asked her to arrange a real exotic weekend with a real woman. Now she had as many male clients with special requests as females. And the best part about it was that everything was anonymous.

"That's great, but I don't know why the men need you, Bettina," Cat said. "There are travel agencies who specialize in that sort of thing."

"Not for the men I deal with. These are high-profile individuals who want complete confidentiality. Since this part of my service caters to the client's personal needs, it's very expensive—and business is booming." She eyed Cat. "You know, I could really use a partner if you ever decide to stop covering the world and find a man of your own."

Cat laughed. "I don't need a nine-to-five business and I don't need a man. You already know that, girl-friend."

They polished off the chips and tacos, finished their drinks and left, splitting in different directions, Bettina to her Honda and Cat to her Harley. At the last minute Bettina turned back. "You know, Cat, maybe I'm wrong about you and Jesse. You're very different but you do have some things in common. He has a motor-cycle. And he seems to be as much a connoisseur of one-night stands as you."

"Forget that. First of all, I'm not interested in one-night stands with anyone I know *personally*." Cat ticked off her fingers. "Second, Jesse already has a job and I've had enough rules and regulations to last a lifetime from my father. And third, unless your brother agrees to audition, I couldn't even put him in the catalog. So what's the point in getting in touch?" She dropped her hands. "No, I'll just have to count on finding some other men who will pose for me."

"It's a tough job..." Bettina laughed. "By the way, how do you find out how your models look in a thong?" she asked curiously.

"Simple. I have all my candidates strip."

JESSE WAS TIRED and he was later than he'd planned. Clouds were building into swirling black shapes across the murky light of the October moon. The breeze was strong. A storm was brewing.

As Jesse picked up speed and let the wind whip past him, he thought about why he loved his motorcycle—it was controlled power. No arguing, just compliance. But driving through a Texas rainstorm changed the rules. The elements didn't abide by the rules. Without order, came chaos. He needed to be careful.

The Katy Highway between Houston and San Antonio alternated from busy clusters of strip malls and fast-food outlets to long flat areas of nothing. He'd been summoned for an appointment in San Antonio with the chief the next morning and Jesse James Dane would never be late. A little caffeine would help; he'd pull into the next truck stop.

In the darkness ahead he caught sight of the tail-lights of an eighteen-wheeler running side by side with a smaller truck.

As he came closer, the commercial rig started to weave and the trucker jerked the vehicle back into his lane. After several "near misses" that forced the pickup to either speed up or slow down, Jesse decided he might be driving into trouble.

Jesse hadn't witnessed a traffic offense in a long time, but it looked as if he was about to. Matters worsened when a light rain began to fall. As Jesse approached, the big rig picked up speed and moved into the passing lane in front of the pickup.

To avoid rear-ending the eighteen-wheeler, the pickup whipped into the inside lane in front of Jesse, forcing him to use his brakes. Normally the bike would have responded but a little sand on a barely wet road caught it and the bike began to slide to the outside lane. For a moment, Jesse thought he had it under control, then the back tire lost traction and the bike skidded into a sudden sideways motion. Jesse swore. He was going to have to lay the bike down. As the eighteen-wheeler that had started the trouble sped out of sight,

Jesse's machine slid across the highway and landed in the ditch with a crunch.

Jesse swore again and pulled himself to a limping stand. Taking a deep breath, he dragged off his helmet, dropped it next to the bike and glanced up to see the pickup driver now backing along the shoulder of the empty highway. He didn't know why the two vehicles had been playing tag and he couldn't assume the driver of the pickup was stopping to be a Good Samaritan. He'd been a ranger long enough to know that even the most innocent action could have disastrous consequences. He stepped back, pulled his cell phone from his backpack, and punched in 9-1-1. No service. Damn. The driver was almost at the crash site. Casually, Jesse reached down and picked up one of the rear view mirrors that had snapped off in the skid.

The vehicle coming to a stop in front of him was no simple pickup. Even in the dark he could see that it was a classic Ford El Camino with some kind of custom-designed toolbox built across the cab's outer wall. As the door opened, the clouds parted and a shaft of moonlight cut through the black rain clouds, hitting the driver like a spotlight and revealing a pair of long, jeans-clad legs, an open stretch of bare midriff and a denim jacket.

"A woman." She peeled off a baseball cap and, with

the shake of her head, her mass of blond hair was caught by the whipping wind.

No, not just a woman, a vision. The Cameron Diaz look-alike strode toward him. She was almost as tall as he was—something he didn't like in a woman. He preferred them tiny and temporary.

"Hello," she called. "Are you okay?"

For a moment he didn't answer. He was struck by an awareness of something very physical between them, an energy that started in his fingertips and vibrated up his arms and into the back of his neck. He could only think it was some kind of atmospheric anomaly caused by the impending storm. He felt as if he was about to be struck by lightning. As a ranger, he'd earned the reputation as Ice Man when he encountered trouble. It kept situations from becoming personal. This time that control seemed totally elusive.

"I'm okay but I might not have been," he blurted, taking his uncertainty out on a woman who didn't deserve it. He couldn't see any lightning but he sure as hell felt electricity in the air. If he'd been standing in water, he'd be fried. It was the kind of feeling he imagined a law officer might experience if he were forced to kill a man.

"Should I have hit him?" she asked, a hint of anger in her voice. He wondered if she felt the tension between them. "I don't think so. My pickup was no match for that big wheeler."

He took another look at the El Camino with the Georgia tag. "Pickup? Not too many normal people drive a restored vehicle like that on the highway."

"I do."

"I can see that." He made a disparaging sound, not so much directed at her as an attempt to disconnect himself from his rescuer. "What's a *woman* from Georgia doing out here alone at this time of night?"

"You have a curfew in Texas for *women* from other states?"

She couldn't see his face. He was a silhouette: a lean, dark figure holding a bike mirror as if it were the head of a staff. The Grim Reaper. All he needed was a cloak and a black horse, Cat mused, shivering. Every nerve in her body responded to him in a way she couldn't understand.

A circle of light split the clouds and fell across the man. She gasped. His five o'clock shadow gave him the sinister look of an old Western outlaw. Dark eyes seemed to look right through her. In response, her teeth began to chatter. She felt as if she were in the eye of a storm. As long as she didn't move, she was safe.

Bettina had asked her who she was waiting for. She'd quipped that she'd know when she found him. One look at the man in the moonlight and she knew he would be at the top of her list. It had been too long since she'd felt such desire and never this intense. She wanted this man naked, in her bed, inside her—and the sooner the better.

The wind picked up, flinging a wet sheen across her face, and she pulled her cap back on, barely aware she was doing it. "I stopped to help you," she said.

"Thanks, but I can manage," he said gruffly.

She took a step back, holding up both hands as a shield. "Okay. Sorry I stopped," she said, annoyed and puzzled at his mood.

He shook his head. "No, I'm sorry. This isn't your fault." If it had been anybody else, he'd have forced himself to be more pleasant, but something he couldn't explain was affecting his breathing. The very air between them was hot.

She asked again, "Are you sure you're all right?"

Those words echoed in his head as he lost himself in thought....

All right? When he was a child, long after his father had gone, he'd asked his mother that. His older brother Mitchell had been forced into becoming the head of the household and making the rules.

Mitchell and Ran, the middle brother, had established a conspiracy of silence that had closed Jesse out, and he'd never understood why. Rule number one was that Mama was sick and Jesse shouldn't go into her room.

Yet, he'd slip into Mama's room when they were away and she would loop her thin arms around him and cry against his chest. "Are you all right?" he'd ask. She'd only cry and say she loved him.

Then came the bad days when she no longer knew him as her youngest son. She'd cried then because she was in pain. He'd continued to break Mitchell's rules— because she'd needed him—until she'd been sent to the nursing home. Then, out of pain and anger, he'd broken some of Mitchell's other rules. On probation from his second DUI charge, Jesse had finished high school one day and joined the marines the next. But he'd never gotten over the feeling that he'd let Mama down.

He'd determined long ago that he'd never let anyone need him again and he'd never break any more rules.

"Listen. I feel bad about what happened," the woman facing him said. "It's starting to rain. If you'll put your bike in the back of my truck I'll drive you wherever you like."

With her hands still extended, his skin tingled with the crazy sensation that she was pushing against him, as though her long fingers were pressed against his bare skin. Damn. When he'd fallen, he must have hit his midsection. The feeling intensified. Hell, he must have hit his head, too.

"No thanks."

"Fine." She dropped her hands and started to turn away, then stopped. "Since you don't want my help, I'll just go."

"Where are you heading?" His question stopped her. He'd surprised himself by asking. Asking made the connection stronger. As the rumble of thunder in the distance grew louder, the physical responses in his body seemed to intensify, fed by the wind and the rain.

"I'm headed for San Antonio. If I read the last road sign right, it's just ahead."

"You're about twenty miles out," Jesse agreed, switching to ranger mode. "It is none of my business, but you shouldn't give out information. In fact, you shouldn't have stopped to help me. Suppose I'm an ax murderer?"

He told himself his voice wasn't tight because of the overwhelming tension that arced between them—he was simply reprimanding her. A smart woman would get out of here. He'd bet she was smart. And gutsy. Whatever she was feeling, she certainly wasn't afraid of him. In fact, he sensed what might be called cynical amusement.

She stood her ground. "I'm just curious. *Are* you an ax murderer or do you club your victims with rearview mirrors?"

He glanced down. He was holding the broken mirror with no recollection of picking it up. "I improvise. What about you?" The words came out as though someone else was speaking. Maybe he really had hit his head.

"Normally, I'd already be gone, but since I did contribute to your accident, I felt compelled to help. It's your call, Motorcycle Man. We can put your bike in the back of the El Camino and get out of the elements or I'll send someone from the next open garage." She jutted her chin forward and waited.

He shook his head. "If I thought the two of us could lift a five-hundred-pound machine into the bed of your truck, I might agree." He didn't have a choice. He'd have to take his chances and let her help. "Just send a wrecker when you get to the next garage."

"Well, I could, but it happens that I have ramps, a tarp and a tool chest in the back. I travel alone so I'm always prepared. By the way, I believe your motorcycle is a Road King and they weigh closer to seven hundred and twenty-five pounds."

Jesse was amazed. She was right about the bike. It was a Harley Road King and it weighed seven hundred and twenty-three pounds. Before he realized what he was doing, he heard himself saying, "I accept your offer. You carry ramps around?"

"They're useful in moving things in and out of the

truck. Never know what I'll need when I start a new assignment."

Because of her tool chest, getting the bike into the truckbed wasn't easy. By the time they'd done it and picked up the broken pieces of metal along the roadside, both were soaking wet. He was still curious about the ramps as he watched the woman pull off her jacket and wet cap, open the passenger side door and lean inside the cab. Moments later she straightened again. "Okay, get in, unless you'd rather ride in the back with the bike. Be careful of my gear on the floor."

Jesse crawled in, carefully planting his feet around the bulky backpacks and wondering how he'd gotten himself into such a situation. The seat shifted as she got in on her side. He turned to thank her and heard a sharp intake of breath, not certain whether it had come from him or her. At this close proximity, they had their first clear view of each other. If tension could be measured by a thermometer, it would have hit the top of the gauge.

With the moonlight behind her, he'd only gotten a general impression of his angel of mercy. Up close, she was straight out of a fantasy comic book. Blond hair streaming in wet ropes and a T-shirt plastered against full breasts, she could have ridden a wild stallion with Zena or been an agent in the next episode of "Silk

Stalkings." If she stepped on a stage with Madonna or Brittany Spears, they'd fade away.

As they continued to eye each other, he took a deep breath and let it out. "Something wrong?" Wrong? If he asked himself that question, he'd have to answer yes. Something was wrong. The woman. The night. The storm.

She simply stared at him, the silence heavy between them. Her voice was tight when she answered. "Maybe. Maybe not. I think I'm just a little shaky. The accident was a shock."

"That surprises me. I'd expect the *average* woman to be shaken up, but the *average* woman doesn't drive a truck carrying tools and equipment."

"Women have toys. They just aren't always what you expect," she said, and closed her door. Mercifully, the light went out. Moments later the engine came to life and she pulled back onto the highway. "It isn't the accident that bothered me. It's you."

"I bother you? Why is that?" he asked.

"I don't know. Men are my business. I've seen all kinds and I've learned to read them. Everything about you says danger."

He didn't know which comment bothered him the most, her reference to danger or that men were her business. He shifted his feet, wondering what she carried in her cases. With a taste for classic vehicles and motorcycles, she had to have money. Or maybe *she* was the ax murderer and she carried her weapons in her cases. Either way, this woman was trouble and trouble was something he didn't need. He was going to find enough of that in the morning at the meeting scheduled with his boss.

"You're very direct for a woman," he finally said. "Or a man, for that matter."

"I believe in confronting a situation head-on, yes." She glanced at him. "I'm curious. You don't seem to be the kind of man who would willingly ask for help, especially from a woman. And I'm definitely not myself around you, either. Can you say there isn't something strange happening here?"

"No, I guess I can't," he admitted. He'd accused her of being direct and he liked that about her. Although if anyone had asked, he would have said it was what he'd always thought he'd wanted in a woman. But now he wasn't so sure. "I don't understand this, either," he said. "Let's just say, there was an accident and it shook us up, and leave it at that."

The windows had fogged, giving the illusion of a gauzy cocoon isolating them from the rest of the world. The air felt warm and unstable.

"Whatever you say." She reached for the windshield defroster. He was right. They were tuned into each other in a way she hadn't experienced before. She attributed her reaction to the fact that he was absolutely perfect for her catalog, but this personal...connection was volatile and disturbing. She felt like the woman who knew there was an ax murderer in the basement. Everything about her said, Don't go down there. And she was heading for the basement as fast as she could.

Cat shrugged her shoulders, trying to break out of what felt like a physical force field. "I prefer to think we're two ships that pass in the night. From the looks of this weather, we could use a ship."

Rain was blowing everywhere now, making it difficult to see. In addition to the weather, her windshield wipers were behaving erratically. Her passenger leaned back, not speaking. If he was worried about her ability to drive in the storm, he didn't say it. Either he was the rare man who could relax with a woman at the wheel or he was scared speechless. She took a quick look. He didn't look scared.

"You can just drop me off anywhere," he finally said.

"If I'd been going to drop you off *anywhere*, you might just as well have stayed where you were. You're soaking wet. I'm soaking wet. And your bike is wrecked. I'll take you home. I suppose it's too much to hope that you live on the River Walk."

"You live on the River Walk?" he asked.

She laughed. "Live? Not likely. Home for me is

wherever my work is. For the next few weeks, home is the Palace Hotel, compliments of my employer—that is, if he's satisfied with my work when we meet."

Satisfied? The Palace Hotel? That was the most expensive hotel on the Walk. Whatever she was, she was being very well paid. "Slow down. We're almost there. Turn left at the next road and be careful as you cross the bridge—there's a low spot on the other side. I live behind the church."

She turned off the highway and drove over the bridge. Her headlights flashed on the church ahead. "Well, I've been with a lot of men, but this is a first."

"Been with a lot of men? Are you always so candid?"

"In my business, I have to be." She shook her head. "Here I am picturing you in your underwear and I find out you're a priest."

Picturing him in his underwear? Satisfied a lot of men? That's when it hit him. She was a hooker, a high-priced call girl. And she thought he was a priest. He couldn't hold back a laugh. "A priest? Not me. I just rent the little house in back. I like the solitude."

"You already told me you weren't an ax murderer so I guess I'll trust you on that." She looked him up and down without seeming conscious of the gesture. "Although I don't know if trusting you is a smart idea."

She returned her eyes to the road. With every bump, the tension grew.

He could smell the rain, the leather of his pants, the hint of flowers that seemed to come from her hair.

As they reached the church, lightning suddenly split the sky, revealing a very old adobe structure with a tiny steeple and a fenced yard. She jumped at the flash of light and laughed self-consciously. "I've seen a lot of chapels like this in my travels," she said, "though seldom illuminated by the hand of God himself! Are we being warned, do you think?"

He was beginning to wonder the same thing. In spite of the defroster, the windshield was still fogging and the wipers had slowed to a jerky crawl. The El Camino and the wipers hesitated at the same time lightning struck again. His nerve endings were vibrating like danger flags caught in the wind.

The engine died and the headlights went out.

"Damn!" his driver swore. "I can't believe this. First your bike wrecks and now my wheels have died. What's next?" She gestured to the sky. "And who knows how long this storm will last."

"As far as I know, we aren't expecting a hurricane, so I'd say it'll blow itself out pretty quick. We can call your...friend at the Palace. I'm sure he can send someone after you, or I'll be glad to drive you when the storm stops. I don't want to hold you up."

She took a deep breath. "That won't be necessary. I'll manage. I truly am sorry if I caused you to go off the road. But you aren't responsible for me. Once the engine cools down, it'll run fine."

He'd turned *her* down when she'd first offered her help. He should have insisted that she go. He hadn't. Now he had a woman on his hands he'd like nothing more than to get his hands on. "You may know your cars but you don't understand about Texas. This is flatland out here. A hard rain and the low areas flood. I think you're stuck for a while."

A crack of thunder emphasized the danger of the storm.

She shivered and he had an almost overwhelming urge to slide his arms around her narrow waist. "You're probably right. My Ellie has a mind of her own."

"Ellie?"

"That's what I call the El Camino. When something isn't right, she just stops until it is. Which is pretty much what I do. Tell you what, if you have any coffee, I'd love a cup—particularly if you have a little brandy to spike it with," she said, running her tongue over her lips.

"No brandy," he said, trying to adjust his lower body, which had started to take on a life of its own. If he sat here, his thigh touching hers any longer, he would incinerate. "Only beer or coffee. But just sit tight a minute. I'll unload the bike before we go inside."

"I'll help," she said as she opened her door, which was immediately caught by the wind.

If there had been any dry spots left on their clothing, there were none by the time they got the bike into his shed.

Finally he replaced her ramps inside the truckbed and started toward his small adobe house. The woman hesitated.

"Come on in, dry off and wait for the rain to stop." Jesse unlocked his door and stood aside. His guardian angel eyed him uncertainly, then moved past him. A sharp pang ran through him as she entered. It was a cardinal rule: when he spent time with a woman it was at her house or on neutral ground and he always went home before morning. Now, he'd let a stranger inside.

But this was different, he told himself. She didn't know his name. And he didn't know hers.

"I don't have a clothes dryer," Jesse said, "but I'll build a fire and you can get warm."

Warm? If she felt the way he did, she'd be better off if he turned on the air conditioner. As he walked over to the corner and crouched in front of an adobe fireplace, Cat sat on a stool and removed her boots.

Moments later flames were licking at the wood. Satisfied that the fire was burning, he stood. "I'm going to get out of this wet shirt and make the coffee," he said. "The bathroom is through that door. There are towels on the shelf."

Cat let out a sigh of relief and headed for the door. The bathroom made her smile. A large claw-footed tub filled almost the entire room. On one wall were shelves filled with towels and...rocks. She supposed he must collect them. Her host was obviously a man of the earth. At least he wasn't a man of the cloth—which was good, considering the way she was feeling. She lifted a towel and turned to go back out to the fire when she spotted a blue flannel shirt hanging on the back of the door. It was soft and dry and smelled like sage, the same smell she'd been so conscious of in the truck. She took in the scent and felt it fuel the fire crackling inside her skin. Moments later, after shedding all her wet clothes, she was snuggled inside the flannel shirt that almost reached her knees.

"Did you find what you needed?" her mystery man asked, rounding the corner into the bathroom and coming to an abrupt stop only inches away from her. At her inadvertent yelp, he apologized. "Sorry. I see you found something to wear."

"If you need your shirt, I'll take it off," she offered, reaching for the top button, then stopped. She'd be completely nude.

"No, that's okay. It looks much better on you."

"It's very soft," she said, sliding her fingers up and down the flannel fabric. "It feels...good."

Jesse let out a deep, hot breath. She seemed to be sending him an invitation, but he couldn't be sure. He desperately tried to hold on to his last thread of control. Then he saw the top of her breasts peeking out the vee of the shirt. She was every man's wet dream. The thread snapped.

He groaned and reached for her.

"Don't," she said, her voice low and tight.

He kissed her.

Silently, hungrily, she responded with such passion that it scared him. She kept her eyes open as he slid his hands beneath the shirt. He started for a moment when he touched her bare hips, then moved slowly upward and cupped her breasts. He felt the pounding of her heart as she slid her arms around his neck and melted against him. He tore his lips away for a moment. "Are you sure about this?"

"That I want you? Absolutely! That it's smart? Not at all. Now, stop talking and make love to me."

He lifted her in his arms.

2

BETWEEN KISSES they were soon naked and breathless on his bed, covered with a down comforter that gathered them close and cushioned them in warmth.

He plunged his hands into her hair, pulling it, kneading her scalp as his hot breath brushed her skin. His lips captured hers in great hungry gulps while his hips ground against her, his arousal pulsating with need. The power of his appetite demanded that she meet his every move with equal fire. She did.

Suddenly he pulled her hands above her head so that she couldn't move. His mouth moved down her neck, tasting her nipple with his tongue and finally capturing it with his lips. Beneath him she writhed, trying desperately to entice him inside her. But he was not finished with her yet. With a hard tug she pulled away from his grasp. Hands free to touch, she explored hard muscles. Soft, pliable skin clenched in its wild need to be joined. Skin against skin, she was on fire, little sparks exploding outward, heating them both, making her wet with want. She knew he could tell she was with him. Pleasure throbbed inside her, growing stronger, frantic to be released.

Jesse was inside her and for a moment any thought of control was gone, until he realized what was happening and forced himself to still. "Whoa, lady," he said in a tight voice. What was he doing, making love to her without protection? And why hadn't she stopped him?

"What's wrong?" she asked.

Everything. Because professional call girl or not, he wanted her.

She squirmed beneath him, crying out with need. He wanted her and he'd gone too far to turn back, but if he was going to break his own code of ethics, he'd still be smart enough to protect himself and her.

He reached past her and fumbled in the drawer in the nightstand. He couldn't reach it and had to lift himself up.

"Don't go away," she said.

He tried to open the packet, dropped it and cursed. The throb grew stronger as if liquid lightning pulsed through his veins.

"You don't need that," she gasped.

"You may not, but I do. I don't take chances." He grabbed the packet from the floor.

"Give it to me," Cat said, pushing him to his back as she removed the contents and tossed the foil to the floor. She smiled. He didn't have to worry, but a little interruption like this always heightened the tension. She slowly rolled the latex down. He moaned and she could feel the muscles in his body contract as she touched him.

"For God's sake, get it done," he growled.

"For my sake, I'm trying."

"Let me." He pushed her away, finished and moved back over her. Their eyes were only inches apart. Even in the dark he could see the same desire he knew she saw in his. She breathed in the air he breathed out. He felt as though he'd never been so close to a woman before. She made a desperate sound deep in her throat and reached between them to grasp the hard length of him. This time she clasped her legs around his body and forced him inside her. There was no thinking, only her woman smell, his smell and the slight salty taste of her skin. He filled her with the raw sense of his hot sex.

This time there was no stopping. This time he slammed into her and she raised herself to meet him. He heard her gasp for breath, crying out in pleasure. He felt the beginning of her climax and tightened his muscles in an effort to sustain the moment, then groaned and once again plunged deep inside her as release exploded through them both.

Jesse had some earth-stopping climaxes before, but never like this. As the tremors subsided, little sparks of aftershocks continued to fire. He lay there until his heart stilled and his breathing went back to near normal. Then, finally, he rolled off her, pulled her close beside him, and curled his arm around her shoulder.

"I don't know what to say," he murmured, no longer loving her with his lips or his hands, yet still connected to her more intimately than he'd thought possible. How could he explain what had happened, how he'd broken his own rule, first about making love to a woman in his own house, then about the kind of woman he'd just shared the most intimate experience of his life with? It had to be an effect of the storm.

"Talking after something like that would be a sacrilege."

"But women like to talk."

"Not this woman. That kind of climax is worth a thousand words and I don't know one that would accurately describe it."

He kissed her forehead, his fingertips drawing little circles on her shoulder, memorizing the feel of her.

"Neither do I."

He continued to hold her as he listened to the sound of his breathing, her breathing, and the heated waves of silence.

She shivered and said, "I think it's stopped raining."

"Are you cold?" he asked, but made no effort to pull up the covers.

"No. Cold is the last thing I am."

"You shivered."

"I think it's because this is a little awkward. I've never been in exactly this situation before."

"What kind of situation?"

"This may happen to you all the time, but I generally don't end up naked in the arms of a man I don't know."

"You don't? You did say men were your business, didn't you?"

"But that's different," she started to explain, then stopped. He wouldn't understand. He was right. She made her living off men's bodies. She even sampled their attributes once in a while. But her partners always knew that it was casual and temporary. By staying in his arms, she'd broken one of her own rules tonight.

"I know. You do your thing, then move on and it's all over." He couldn't pretend he expected anything else. From the beginning, everything about her looks, clothes, those heart-attack legs said big bucks and the expertise to demand it.

"Well, yes."

"So this is over?" His words came out before he had known what he was going to say.

"Certainly. I mean, why wouldn't it be?"

"Business as usual?" he said, wondering why he

was bothered by her statement. He agreed with her. Didn't he?

"Well, no. This isn't business," she admitted, a curious catch in her voice. "It's personal. Normally, I make it a point to enjoy each...encounter, recognize it for what it is and move on. But this is different." She was beginning to get a strange feeling about what was happening between them. "Like you said, I'm a direct woman. Since I'm being honest, I'll confess I wanted you like I've never wanted any man. And you wanted me. How does that make you feel?"

"Horny as hell," he admitted. "This was possibly a mistake, yet I'm about one touch away from making another."

She laughed dryly. "Well, at least you're man enough to admit when you've made a mistake."

"And to admit when I've broken a few of my own rules."

"Maybe we both did."

The warm cocoon was dissipating. Cat didn't like the awkward feeling. Always before, she and her partner had been on the same page. Tonight neither she nor her one-night stand had taken the lead and the result felt like two pieces of wire still sparking but no longer connected. It was time to go, before she did or said something dumb like "Can I live with you and have your children?"

Finally she made an uneasy move away. When he didn't pull her back, she said the first thing that came to mind. "You think that coffee's ready?"

"I'm sure it is," he said, then stood and held out his hand to help her up. "By the way, if this *were* a business arrangement and I wanted to hire you, what would you have said to me?"

She stood, slid her arms into his flannel shirt, gathered up her damp clothes and headed to the fire in the other room, trying to put some distance between her and the man who'd just ravished her gloriously. "You don't understand. It's me that would be hiring you. And, that's easy. I would have started by asking you to strip. Then I'd make you an offer."

She didn't know why she'd said that. That was her wise-cracking, break-the-ice line for models. But this wasn't a wise-cracking kind of man. Suddenly she was confused. She had to get dressed and leave. Granted, her El Camino was low to the ground. Granted, the flat areas of Texas flooded quickly. Granted, he wasn't an ax murderer. And he hadn't done anything she hadn't wanted. In fact, he'd done exactly what she'd wanted. Yet, she had the urge to run.

She heard him pad to the kitchen. Then she grabbed her clothes out of the bathroom, and as she leaned down and pulled on her jeans, she caught the scent of him again—as if he'd just removed his shirt and handed it to her. With nervous energy she crossed her arms over her chest and hugged the fabric close. For a long moment she held her breath, then let it out, chastising herself for being bewitched—for that was the only excuse she could come up with for how she was feeling. Clasping the towel with both hands, she leaned her head forward and began rubbing her wet hair.

"Coffee's ready. Sorry, it's black." Wearing a pair of worn jeans, riding low on his hips, and a University of Texas T-shirt, he was carrying two mugs.

He walked over to her chair, handed her one, then moved toward the television. "Hope you don't mind, but I want to catch the news." He turned on the television and collapsed in his easy chair as if nothing had happened between them. Flipping channels, he seemed to focus all his attention on the news reports as if she wasn't there. Was he finding this as strange as she was? Was he going to ignore her reply about stripping?

Moments later he was totally involved in the story of the solving of a five-year-old case, an undertaker who'd killed his wife and buried her in the same casket as the elderly aunt of one of San Antonio's leading citizens. At the time, the undertaker appeared to be grief stricken. With no body or evidence to support foul play, the police had been forced to release him. The mortician's wife had disappeared. Only the determined efforts of a Texas Ranger had finally solved the case. The problem was, he'd neglected to get permission from the family whose plot he'd disturbed.

Cat stood and walked over to the fireplace. The rain had stopped. It was time she left. As she turned to tell him, she noticed a desk in the corner and the pictures under the glass top. They appeared to be his family. Boys playing football. A girl hugging a guy.

No, not just a guy, it was the man she'd just made love with. He was wearing a white Stetson and a badge.

The woman was Bettina Dane.

"Now, for a word with the officer," the television reporter was saying. Cat turned to the TV and watched him walk toward a tall, dark man wearing the customary white shirt and white Stetson worn by the Texas Rangers. "He's the newest member of the San Antonio unit and he's setting a remarkable record. A champion of law and order, he's being called San Antonio's supercop. Excuse me, Ranger—"

Cat leaned forward. She recognized that silhouette.

"—Jesse James Dane. Could we have a word with you?"

"No comment," was the icy reply as he turned away.

Jesse James Dane. Bettina's brother. The very man she'd planned to avoid. Suddenly a click changed the station to the weather channel where the forecaster was informing the public that the possibility of flooding was not over.

Jesse turned and saw that she'd witnessed the news clip. "I think I'd better go," she said.

She watched Jesse take a big swig from his mug, give an elaborate shrug of his shoulders and lean back. "Relax. You're safe from arrest. I'm off duty. Besides, the storm may be past, but you never know about flooding. Until we're sure, you're welcome to stay."

"No!" Cat handed Jesse her mug and babbled like an idiot. "I have to get into town. Mr. Szachon is expecting me. I'll get your shirt back to you. I'll be able to buy you a new bike if this job goes well."

Jesse stared at her. Sterling Szachon. He should have known. Everything about her said *high-priced*. From the beginning she'd been honest—she was out of his league. She was also a woman who gave full value for her service. He could attest to that. But her announcement that she was meeting Sterling Szachon knocked him for a loop.

As rich as Donald Trump, as handsome as sin, Szachon had taken San Antonio by storm. Like Trump, he had a reputation for success with both business and the ladies. He had a new female companion at his side every six months. The gossip was that they were all informed they were temporary. When their time was up, he'd give them something very expensive and send them happily on their way. The gossip didn't say the women were professionals, but this mystery woman with the El Camino had said he would be her employer. He couldn't blame her for keeping her profession private with her quip that *she* did the hiring, but he couldn't stop a pang of regret. He stood and took a step toward her.

"Keep the shirt. And you're not responsible for my bike. I have insurance."

"Thank you for the shirt," she said formally.

"Thank you for driving me home," he murmured just as stiffly, following her as she backed out the kitchen door, stepped into a puddle of water and skidded.

He caught her elbows and she was in his arms again. There was an odd moment where both were absolutely still. By the light in the kitchen, he could see the clear blue of her eyes fringed by brown-gold lashes. He felt her catch her breath and hold it.

He'd thought he was in control. Since the death of his mother, he'd spent ten years training himself to erase emotion. Love hurt once it was gone. And this was a love-'em-and-leave-'em woman. But as she slowly let out the air in her lungs, he leaned forward and kissed her again. Like a lover, not a stranger. He hadn't known he was going to do it.

For a second Cat parted her lips, then moaned and pulled away, her eyes open wide in surprise.

"Why did you do that?" she asked, her voice a throaty whisper.

"You're in Texas," he said. "people here kiss hello and goodbye."

"I...h-have to go," she stammered, pushing out of his arms and dashing to her truck.

He opened his mouth, then closed it. He didn't know her name. He didn't want to. It was better that way.

THE EL CAMINO'S ENGINE started, just as she'd said. From the way she sped away, it was clear that if she had to, she'd swim to get away from him. As a man, he knew he ought not to go after her. As a Texas Ranger who had caused her desperate need to run, he told himself he couldn't *not* go. She didn't have to know. He'd just tag along behind her to make certain that she made it into town.

He watched as her truck sputtered a bit. But she was a good driver and made it onto the bridge. His vehicle, a Dodge Ram, rode across the water like a big sleek boat. He kept his distance, allowing her the illusion of being alone—at least until they reached the hotel. He slowed his truck as she drove onto the mock draw-bridge entrance to the Palace, unloaded her luggage, then handed the keys over to the valet. Szachon had built a place that rivaled the Taj Mahal. If there'd been a ten-star rating, this hotel would get an eleven. The high-priced call girls he'd known about couldn't afford to operate out of the Palace unless they were invited. This woman had a personal invitation.

With her long, determined stride she headed for the revolving doors, then stopped and turned back, her eyes scanning the street as if she sensed his presence. For just a second they seemed to connect on some level and he felt an odd tingle, then she tilted her chin up and entered the hotel.

He drove across the ramp, lowered the passenger window so that he could see her pause briefly at the registration desk then be whisked away toward the elevators without registering. Obviously she was expected.

What the hell was wrong with him, following this woman? He already had an appointment with his captain in the morning for what was certain to be a dressing-down. Getting a judge's permission to disturb a grave without knowledge of the family had solved the crime, but he hadn't followed political protocol. In his mind, the end result justified the means since he'd managed to solve a case. But he'd put a question mark in his file.

A Texas Ranger often operated alone, but he was expected to use good judgment. Jesse knew the captain wouldn't gloss over his actions, even though he'd found the murdered woman and made the arrest. All he could do was apologize to the grieving family of the woman whose grave he'd opened.

He understood about grief and loss, and he'd found his own way to survive. First the marines, then later the Texas Rangers. They'd become his family, his stability in a life that had been an angry rebellion. Each had provided boundaries and taught him the value of rules. Now, he'd not only broken a department rule, he'd broken a personal one, as well.

Tomorrow he'd accept his captain's punishment. Tonight, watching the most incredible woman he'd ever made love to disappear into another man's territory was punishment enough.

AS THE ELEVATOR Cat and the Palace bellman shared shot up the side of the lobby, she was only vaguely aware of the luxurious hotel decor. Her mind seemed to be fused to a simple adobe house behind the church. From riding a Harley in the rain to fussing over the weather, everything about Jesse James Dane had been a contradiction. They'd shared incredible sex, then he'd turned away, glued to a newscast.

Normally she picked men that were easy to define. But this time she hadn't picked. This time she'd been slammed into him thanks to a storm and her instincts to be a Good Samaritan. At least he didn't know she was a friend of his sister Bettina's.

As the elevator slowed Cat forced herself to concentrate on the man she was about to meet. Sterling Szachon was expecting her. He'd pay her well and provide living quarters and a liberal expense account. In return, she'd select the sites and photograph the models for his male underwear catalog. To make that happen, she'd forget about Jesse James Dane, Texas Ranger, trouble in every sense of the word.

At least he didn't know her name.

THE ELEVATOR DOOR slid open with a whisper. She realized that they were exiting into a private corridor. The bellman wheeled his cart past the main set of double doors down the corridor and unlocked a smaller door.

Cat entered the room, caught sight of the elaborate fruit bowl and flower arrangement and knew immediately that this had to be a temporary arrangement. No catalog photographer was provided with such luxurious surroundings.

"Are you certain this is where I'm supposed to be?" she asked.

"Oh, yes, ma'am. Mr. Szachon left instructions for us to take you to your room. The top floor houses his personal living quarters, his office and his executive staff.

He owns the hotel, you know." He unloaded her bag and camera equipment, adjusted the drapes, pointed out the television and gave her the special elevator key needed to reach the top floor. She gave him a tip and he excused himself.

Well, maybe, she decided, but until she met Mr. Szachon she would leave her bags packed. This room made her uneasy. Until she signed the contract, this wasn't a done deal. And staying in her employer's quarters was unacceptable, even if the rest of the staff did enjoy the same privilege. She made a list of what she needed, including a sample case of his underwear and an assistant, preferably female.

By ten o'clock she'd eaten the fruit. By midnight she reined in her frustration at being ignored, pulled off everything but the flannel shirt and her panties, and went to bed. She'd get a good night's rest and meet with the underwear king in the morning at her convenience.

But sleep was elusive. She tossed and turned, trying to empty her mind of distractions. It wasn't her meeting with Szachon but her physical collision with Jesse Dane that kept intruding. He simply marched into her mind and took control.

He hadn't taken anything she hadn't given, but nothing about their lovemaking had been ordinary. It was almost as if she had been the victim of one of those fancy new drugs but she'd had nothing to eat or drink and she didn't have to be told that Jesse was true-blue and full of propriety. Jesse was a ranger and by definition, followed the rules. A man like that tended to be her least favorite type, unless the man was following her rules.

And she hadn't set any.

She hated to admit it but no man had ever affected her so strongly. Her body still strummed its need for more. She didn't understand the lingering aftermath of heat.

She understood control. It was something her father had valued. Control was a state of mind, a kind of self-protection for someone who lived by the book. There were rules of order and, just as her father had done, she was certain Jesse kept every one of them. Except where women were concerned. Apparently he had different standards for one-night stands with perfect strangers. Still, like her, the ranger seemed to be out of sync at the end. Considering he lived by the rules, she was surprised he hadn't escorted her back to the hotel. For a moment there, she'd been disappointed that he hadn't.

Cat forced her attention away from Jesse James Dane to the man who was hiring her, Sterling Szachon, nicknamed Zon by the press when they dubbed him one of the twenty-five richest bachelors in the world. Cat had done a little research of her own. The press could well be right. Mr. Szachon owned a large, successful hotel chain, a major league baseball team, real estate, at least one ranch and a local Texas cable service. But the thing that made him different was that people seemed to genuinely like Zon. With his golden opulence, the women certainly did.

He had the Midas touch; every new project turned to gold. She could only hope that his underwear business followed that pattern. Shooting his catalogs would be a feather in her cap. And though she'd never admit it to Bettina, she was ready to stay in one spot for a while—so long as she had her photography to use as her get out-of-jail card when she wanted to go.

Finally she began to relax. Sleep would come. But it wouldn't be Sterling Szachon who invaded her dreams, it would be a dark-haired Texas Ranger wearing jeans low on his hips, an Ice Man who slept under a down comforter, a man whose kiss still seared her lips.

Cat was aware of the sudden slowing of her breath. Of the shimmering reminder of what she'd shared with a stranger. She took a great gulp of air and breathed in the ever-present scent of Jesse that still clung to his shirt. With a moan of loss, she caught hold of the sheet and pulled it up to her chin.

Her last thought before she fell asleep was, What the hell happened to her?

3

THE INSISTENT RING of the phone roused Cat from a deep sleep. It took her a minute to remember where she was: the employee quarters of Sterling Szachon's penthouse suite.

She reached for the receiver. "Hello?"

"Ms. McCade, this is Austin, Mr. Szachon's executive assistant. Mr. Szachon would like you to join him for breakfast in his quarters."

Cat sat up and glanced at the clock—7:00 a.m. "Breakfast?"

"Yes, ma'am. Will thirty minutes be enough time for you to get ready?"

"It won't take me that long."

Still wearing Jesse's shirt, she pulled on a dry pair of jeans, brushed her teeth and ran a brush through her hair. The last stroke of the brush brought her palm to the collar of Jesse's flannel shirt. She tilted her head, pulled the fabric to her nose and inhaled a deep breath. Now the shirt smelled like both of them. Funny what turned a woman on. Maybe she was crazy but this time it wasn't just a man's body she smelled—the scent triggered a memory, pulling her back to the night they'd shared. There ought to be other memories like that, memories of shared pleasure with other men. But there were none that mattered.

Until Jesse. And that had to stop. Always before, she'd walked away. This time she couldn't. This time she didn't want to go. This time she was scared.

But business before pleasure. "Remember, Cat, your business *is* your pleasure. You just have an itch you haven't quite scratched yet." If her boss wanted to call a business meeting in his quarters, she could wear the flannel shirt.

She tossed the brush on the counter, pulled on her running shoes and headed for the door. The penthouse corridor was empty. As she reached the end of the corridor, the door opened and a grandfatherly looking man with silver hair stood there. "I'm Austin, Ms. McCade. This way, please." Through a glass window off the foyer, she could see a table set for a meal. Beside it stood the man she recognized as her potential employer.

The reports were accurate. Sterling Szachon, barechested and wearing sleek, blue workout shorts, was blond, tanned, and muscular. A compact man with a scar on his leg, he looked much too normal to carry the reputation he'd amassed. Instead, he seemed more like the guy next door, the kind your mother wanted to take you to the prom. She couldn't help thinking that Jesse Dane would have been the bad boy. With the towel across his shoulder, Zon was wiping his forehead and drying the back of his neck.

"Sorry. I've been working out. Ms. McCade, come have a seat and talk to me about men's bodies." He grinned. "From your catalogs I can see you're an expert."

He didn't waste any time. She looked around. She'd been criticized for not wasting any time, either, but she learned early on that she'd had to set the rules. "Mr. Szachon, I hope you won't be offended, but I didn't expect a man in your position to be so...informal."

He smiled. "What's wrong with being informal?"

"Absolutely nothing. I'm sorry. I just don't usually conduct my business in this kind of setting. Why don't you enjoy your breakfast and I'll meet you afterward in your office?"

This time he laughed. "I'm sorry. I try to meet with my associates in the morning to plan my day. I find my mind is sharper before I clutter it up with details. My staff is used to my informality but if it makes you uncomfortable, I understand. Let me make it quick.

"I'm a man who likes to have a hand in my projects. I've been told that you work alone. I just wanted to meet you in person so that we can decide whether or not we can work together before I get called away to something else. I've already checked your references and seen samples of your catalog photographs. Not only that, but a business associate gave you high marks for integrity."

"A business associate? Who?"

"You know, I have no idea what her last name is. I e-mail her and tell her what I need and she gets it done. I've never even seen her. She operates a business called Rendezvous. Calls herself Bettina."

Cat was stunned. Bettina's newest venture. Getaways and gewgaws for wealthy men. She'd even admitted she'd heard of Sterling Szachon, yet had failed to say he was a client. "I just saw Bettina two days ago. She didn't mention knowing you."

"One of the conditions of our business arrangement is that it remains confidential. She was, however, very complimentary of your work. Your ability to separate your business and your personal life was a trait that appealed to me, considering you photograph men. I ought to tell you that you'll actually be working for my sister, Elizabeth. This will be her project. As I said, I've read your proposal and drawn up a contract empowering you to design the catalog." He handed her a file. "Take it with you and look it over. We'll meet again in my office in about thirty minutes and decide."

Cat took the folder. Design the catalog? She hadn't expected that much authority. Working with the tycoon and his sister might be a problem, but she'd always found ways to make things work. This project was what she'd been waiting for. "Can you arrange for me to get samples of your products?"

"Of course." He nodded and Austin appeared to accompany her back to her room. The contract was even more generous than she'd expected. Sterling Szachon's job was the offer she'd been waiting for. She was excited, yet vaguely troubled. Bettina's recommendation was appreciated, though her involvement with Szachon was a surprise. Cat couldn't help but think about Bettina's habit of playing matchmaker to her friends.

What was just as unreal was that in a state as big as Texas, Cat had inadvertently caused a stranger to wreck his bike and that stranger turned out to be Bettina's brother Jesse James Dane. She still didn't know how that happened. Perhaps Bettina's name ought to be listed as "consultant to the stars"—specifically for Kevin Bacon. Cat was willing to bet that it wouldn't take Bettina *Six Degrees of Separation* to connect to any single man or woman in the South.

Cat suddenly felt like the filling in an Oreo cookie sandwich. She was caught between a very powerful man who had expected her to help him fulfill his high expectations and a Texas Ranger who'd already compromised her ability to keep her mind on her job.

Thanks to Bettina, Cat's life was spiraling out of control. And she didn't like it.

JESSE MADE A QUICK CHECK of the chapel to look for storm damage, climbed into his truck and headed for town. He glanced at the clock on the dash and pressed the gas pedal. The captain might be unhappy with Jesse's methodology in finding the murdered woman's body, but a killer was behind bars.

Twenty minutes later his worst fears were realized when Captain Wade said grimly, "I am aware that a Texas Ranger never closes a case until he gets his man, Jesse, but you stirred up a bit of controversy when you went straight to Judge Harris for a search warrant without either my permission or that of the vice-mayor's family."

"You were in Austin," Jesse said, "and I got word our man, the mortician, was about to relocate some of the grave sites, including the one where he'd stashed his wife's body. Technically, there was no point in notifying the family that I was exhuming a body, if the body was being exhumed anyway. I just needed permission to open the casket. I figured that if I was wrong, there was no point in stirring up people who were still grieving. Even Judge Harris agreed."

"It didn't work. As a professional courtesy, the funeral home director called the vice-mayor. By that time, you'd already found the murdered woman's body in the casket beneath. The mayor isn't a happy cowboy this morning, Jess, and his assistant didn't accept my apology. He spoke to the governor, who feels you should be taken off active duty while you take a refresher course in legal procedure. And he thought it wouldn't hurt for you to work on your people skills at the same time. I agreed to both his suggestions."

Both suggestions? Jesse had a bad feeling about where the captain was going when he said, "So, I'm assigning you to one of the mayor's special projects. It will give you a chance to win him over by showing him your people skills. You do have some, don't you?"

"There's nothing wrong with my people skills. I'm fair and honest and trustworthy. I was a Boy Scout, a United States Marine and now I'm a Texas Ranger. I don't think even the mayor can claim that."

"He doesn't have to, Ranger. It was a member of his family whose grave you opened. Take this seriously, Jess. He wants me to nail your Boy Scout butt to the wall."

"I'm prepared to accept whatever disciplinary action you deem proper."

"Fine. You're assigned to the mayor's office where you'll serve as a bodyguard for a businessman who is bringing a great deal of money into San Antonio."

"And who is this person I'm being assigned to?"

"Sterling Szachon, the newest billionaire to call Texas home."

Jesse was stunned. This couldn't be happening. He was being assigned to the same man his mystery woman was... "No way."

"Oh, yes," the captain said. "He's been threatened. Well, not him specifically, but the women he's involved with have been. We don't know yet but we can't take a chance. So you're to report to Mr. Szachon."

The women Szachon is involved with? The woman he'd followed to make sure she was safe was going straight into danger without even knowing it. He felt a cold shiver ripple down his back. "I'm sure Szachon has his own staff of bodyguards. Why does he need me?"

"Maybe I'd better let him explain. We're to meet him in twenty minutes, Jess. So let's go."

"Wait a minute," Jesse protested as they climbed into the patrol car and headed for the Palace. "This is not a good idea. I'll escort little old ladies, kiss babies, even go to every career day in every school in the San Antonio area. But dealing with the rich and famous is not my cup of tea. I'll take the desk job."

"Nope. The mayor is expecting Jesse James Dane." He let out a sigh and turned toward the ranger. "I think this sucks, Jesse, but if we keep Szachon happy, the mayor is happy. If the mayor is happy, he'll forget you poked around in his great-aunt's coffin. Let's go."

That was an order. Restrained, but unquestionably an order. "I'll do what I can but, trust me, this is a waste of taxpayer's money. I'm no billionaire's bodyguard. If catching the bad guys isn't enough to be a good ranger, I don't know what else I can do to prove I'm qualified. I certainly don't think hanging out at the Palace will prove the kind of stuff I'm made of."

"Spend much time at the Palace, do you?"

"No, I don't." He fervently hoped they wouldn't run into his mystery woman.

The captain parked the patrol car in front of the hotel and they headed for the concierge's desk to pick up a key to the executive floor.

As they exited the elevator, Jesse tried to figure out how to get out of what was coming. The captain led the way down the corridor and knocked on the door at the end. It opened, revealing a man dressed in a running suit and Nike joggers. Everything about him said power.

"Come in, Captain Wade." He allowed the captain and Jesse to enter, then planted his gaze on Jesse. "I'm Sterling Szachon."

"Ranger Jesse Dane, sir."

"There have been threats, Dane. The mayor said

he'd find the right man. Did he explain what I want you to do?"

"Not really," Jesse answered. "According to the mayor, you're in some kind of danger. If you'll give us the details, we'll investigate."

"That's not quite right," Szachon said. "There have been threats. What I want is a bodyguard. The mayor recommended you, and I think you'll do just fine. I'll put you on the payroll beginning immediately."

"Sorry, Mr. Szachon, we pay our men," the captain cut in. "You could make a donation to our benevolent fund if you like. In the meantime, I'll leave you to work out the details. Just report back to me, Ranger." The captain doffed his cap and left.

"Fine. Sit down, Dane. What can I tell you?"

Jesse let out a sigh and followed directions. "You've received some kind of physical threat?"

"Not me. It appears this crazy person is only interested in the women around me. He, she, whoever the stalker is doesn't seem to have anything serious in mind. It's more like a cat-and-mouse game and it has spooked my staff. This morning's note said that anyone involved in my SterlingWear project had better watch out."

"Have you talked to the local police?"

"Certainly. They're looking into the person making the threats and my personal security staff is watching

Elizabeth. You're here to accompany Cat McCade, my photographer, who will be searching the public sector for candidates for a clothing catalog. I asked for the youngest, most fit-looking ranger in San Antonio. Whoever is making the threats needs to know that you are a man they don't want to mess with. An added benefit will be that you're local and might know where to find the models for my catalog."

"I'm not sure I'm the right person," Jesse said, more confused than he wanted to let on. He wanted to say that Szachon already knew a woman who was an expert on men. Instead, he said, "I think you need a woman for that job."

"I believe I have someone who fits the bill." He moved to a side door and opened it. "Please come in."

Jesse stood. He knew what was about to happen. He'd felt it from the moment he'd walked into the room. The door opened and the woman who appeared was the blond sex goddess from the night before. And she was still wearing his shirt.

She took one step forward, stopped and looked from Jesse to Szachon and back again. She frowned. "I don't understand."

"I think I'm beginning to," Jesse said. "I assume you *satisfied* Mr. Szachon's expectations."

"Yes, he's offered me the job."

Jesse glared at Ms. McCade. "I guess the old saying is true. Experience always wins."

"I've employed Ranger Dane to be your bodyguard, Ms. McCade. Do you have a problem with him?"

"I'm sorry, Mr. Szachon," Jesse said. "I'm not in the escort business. I'm certain my captain wouldn't have assigned me to you if he'd known what kind of business you were really opening. This is the first time I ever heard of a call-girl business putting out a catalog, but we have a strict policy on prostitution in San Antonio."

Cat's mouth flew open in surprise. Jesse Dane thought she was a call girl. She felt as if all her blood had rushed to her feet.

Szachon frowned. "I think maybe you have the wrong impression. Sit down, Dane," he said, motioning toward the chairs in front of his desk. "You, too, Ms. McCade."

"Come on, Ranger Dane," Cat said, "Call girl? You think I'm a prostitute?" She could tell by his face that he did. She'd told him that men were her business; that was the line she always used, a kind of harmless flirting. It was misleading, but it usually separated the good prospects from the men who wouldn't come alive in front of her camera. Yes, she flirted with them. They didn't seem to mind. She never took it any further, at least not until after the shoot was complete. And she'd never said it to a man she'd just gotten naked with.

Until last night.

Last night she'd fallen into his bed with such total abandon that she was still feeling the aftereffects. She should have explained who she was before she'd run away. And she would have, except she'd seen Bettina's picture and all she'd wanted to do was to escape from the trap she'd fallen into.

Jesse James Dane actually thought she was a call girl? Looking back on her actions, she could even understand. Is that why he seemed so angry? Suddenly she was conscious of the silence. Both men were looking at her with peculiar expressions.

She forced herself to smile and to take a seat. Maybe this was her fault. She'd led him down the wrong path. She hadn't expected to ever see him again, certainly not to be teamed up with him. What should she do? Walk away from the best job of her life? No. She'd find a way to deal with this man. This was business and she was a professional.

Jesse sat in the other chair.

Sterling Szachon took his place behind his desk and looked at them both with veiled eyes. "Is there something going on here I should know about, Ranger Dane?"

"No, sir."

"Good. Now, Dane, this is *not* a call-girl catalog. With Ms. McCade's help, we're going to sell underwear. But it's men's underwear we're selling. And it's male models we want. And your job is to accompany her while she finds and auditions those models for our catalog."

"I'd rather not have him with me," Cat said.

"I apologize," Jesse said stiffly as he stood. "But I believe you'd both be happier with another ranger. Let me talk to the captain." *And right after that, the unemployment office.* He turned and left the room, closing the door with a slam.

Sterling Szachon chortled. "I believe he actually thinks I'm some kind of pimp."

"Only because he thinks I'm a prostitute."

Szachon frowned. "I'm truly sorry about that. I can't imagine where he got that idea. However, Dane could be right. Maybe someone else would be better. I'll call the mayor and request another ranger."

"No," Cat said. "This is my fault. Please, let me straighten it out. I can assure you, I don't need a bodyguard."

"I'm sorry, Ms. McCade, but I am responsible for your safety. I hadn't intended to tell you...but I can see that you're not easily frightened. This is my sister, Elizabeth." He held out a picture of a lovely auburn-haired woman. "Someone has been stalking Elizabeth. The tires on her car have been slashed and she's received threatening notes. She's terrified. I don't think you have anything to worry about, but I insist you have someone with you. I'm sorry Ranger Dane is a problem and I'm certain that the governor will deal with him. It will probably cost him his job."

"No. Don't do that," Cat said, heading for the door.

"Where are you going?"

"After Ranger Dane. Mr. Szachon, I think I'd rather deal with the devil I know than one I don't. Let me talk to him."

She'd already wrecked his bike. Now he was about to become unemployed because of her.

"Ms. McCade!" Szachon called.

"Cat!" she snapped.

"Someone really has been stalking Elizabeth. I warn you, I don't take threats lightly. I have a reputation to protect and I don't want to get into trouble with any of the officials I have to work with—state or city. Selling men's underwear is a legitimate business and I'm determined to make it a success. I'm depending on you to help me sell SterlingWear. If you can't make it happen, I'll find someone else."

There it was, the ultimatum. Trouble? She'd faced that before. But this was different. Either she would be responsible for the ranger losing his job or she would have to work with him.

"I can make it happen." That thought shook her. She left the room, hoping that Ranger Jesse Dane hadn't done anything foolish such as call his captain and resign. Because whether she wanted it or not, he was going to be her bodyguard.

JESSE MADE HIS WAY through the lobby and onto the first empty bench along the Walk. He didn't know what had happened back there. He'd let a woman make him so crazy that he'd just killed his future as a ranger and it wasn't even her fault.

He'd been so rocked by his physical reaction to the woman with whom he'd shared the most incredible night of sex of his entire life that he was about to give up everything he'd worked for. No question about it, his ass was grass. He'd already broken the rules by offending a public official's family even though he'd been trying to save them grief. Now the incredible Cat McCade had come along and was about to lead him down a path of self-destruction. He'd taken a woman he didn't even know, a woman he'd thought was a prostitute, into his house and made love to her.

He could see the headlines; Texas Ranger Charged With Sexual Misconduct...Texas Economy Collapses As Sterling Szachon relocates...Governor Swears Ranger Dane Will Never Work In Law Enforcement Again.

4

CAT FOUND JESSE sitting on a bench beside the river, staring into the water as if it held the answers to the world's problems.

"I didn't think a Texas Ranger ran away from trouble," she said.

"That's where you're wrong, lady. I run real good when I have to. You ought to understand that."

"I never run from trouble."

"Sure you do. That's what you did last night, isn't it?"

He caught her by surprise with that and she remained silent.

"Why did you take off?" he persisted.

She owed him an answer. "Because you're Bettina's brother."

"You know Bettina? I should have known. How'd she work this out?"

"She didn't. She's my friend...I didn't know who you were. Not until...afterward, when I walked over to your desk. I saw her picture, panicked and ran. And just to set the record straight, I am not, nor have I ever been, a hooker. I am a professional photographer. That's how I met Bettina. Once she retired her brother's photographs—yours included—she hired me to shoot her new bachelors. My first solo job. I found I had a talent for photographing men and that's where I'm building my reputation."

"Men are your business," was his terse comment. "You told me that."

"We seem to have a situation here, Ranger. Whether you believe me or not, I am going to find and photograph the models for Mr. Szachon's first catalog. I don't care anything about any threats and I'm not worried. I can do this by myself if I have to, but he won't allow it. I know this is awkward, but if you insist on resigning your job, my honor demands that I do the same."

"Very dramatic." She was good at drama. He could be good, too. "And if I convince you not to resign and you get killed, it's my fault. I lose either way."

"So," she said, "you take the bodyguard job and we both get what we want." Where had that come from? *Get what we want?* What she wanted from Jesse had nothing to do with the job. Another bodyguard was the answer, one who didn't make her want to be in his arms.

"I'm certain that the mayor could request another

ranger. Why would you want me to stay, Ms. Mc-
Cade?"

"This job is important to me and if working with you
is what it takes to make it a success, I can do it. The
truth is, I'd like you to stay because you're good at
what you do."

"Only because I choose what I work on. A Texas
Ranger picks his own cases and this isn't a case I'd take
on."

"Up to you, of course, but you don't seem the type to
take any chances where a woman's safety is concerned." She sat beside him on the bench, felt him
stiffen and lean the other way. That was unacceptable.
She was doing something she never did—apologizing—and he was refusing to meet her halfway. "Fine.
It's your choice. I offered to kiss and make up."

Kiss and make up? He sprang up, walked a few feet,
then stopped. He sucked in a deep breath and nodded
his head. "You're right. I may not like it, but I am
sworn to protect the public."

"A man of rules, that's what Bettina said you were.
Just like my dad, the colonel."

"Rules bother you?"

"No, not the rules, the inflexibility they represent.
Actually, rules are safe. You don't have to think or
make your own decisions. You take orders and you
give them. Everything is black and white."

"You said your father was a military man?" Jesse asked.

"He was. Yours?"

"He was a traveling man. He ran away from rules. He finally ran so far he didn't come back."

"But you don't run," Cat said.

"No, unless you count my running away from Bettina's matchmaking efforts." He walked to the water's edge and looked down. "I just can't figure out how she arranged this."

"She didn't. I'll admit that she told me to look you up. I refused."

"Once my brother Mitchell married Anne, I knew I was in trouble," Jesse went on as if she hadn't spoken. "When Anne's mama and Anne's employer got married, I was bound to be next."

"For goodness' sake, Jesse, haven't you heard a word I said. She didn't arrange this. It just happened."

He finally glanced at her and felt his body tighten. He didn't want to know that the connection between them was still as hot as it had been the night before. It was.

"I don't believe you. However you managed it, you can call Bettina and tell her that, as of now, she's deep in the heart of something and it's not Texas. As for the underwear king, you can tell him the men in Texas don't need catalogs to tell them what to wear. In fact—" he looked her up and down and gave a wicked grin "—most of us don't even wear underwear. You should have figured that out last night."

"I did." She understood why he was angry but she'd told him the truth—most of the truth, anyway. And she'd made concessions that she never made. Still, he was brushing her off. He believed she and Bettina were involved in some kind of conspiracy. He'd been ready to believe that she was a prostitute and now he was convinced that she was in cahoots with Bettina the Matchmaker. She was innocent on both counts. But if she were Jesse James Dane, she probably wouldn't believe her, either.

Unless she stopped him, Jesse was ready to walk away from her, and that hurt in a way she didn't understand. She didn't know why she even cared. He was right about another thing, too. She'd spent a good part of her life running away from men like him. In contrast, he respected the same rules that had given her father the right to put his daughters in a box and to teach them there were limits to what they could do. Her mother had accepted that life; her sisters even relished the security.

But not her. Not Cat McCade. She refused to accept the limits rules implied. Travel was her solace, a physical expression of her freedom. Wanderlust filled her soul with satisfaction. She was in control. And now, finally, just as she was in a position to prove that a woman could live on her own terms, Jesse James Dane had crashed straight into her life.

"All right," she said. "Let's talk about last night. Believe what you will. But I'll admit that I wouldn't have done anything differently. Last night was...well, I don't know what it was. Whatever we want to make it, I suppose. I've learned to accept what comes along because I know it's only temporary, but I'm sorry you're so caught up in your rules that you won't admit that you felt it, too. So, let's make a deal," she went on. "We start over, put last night behind us. You need to protect the women around Mr. Szachon to keep your job and I need to do this catalog to cement my reputation. The job will only last a few weeks, then we'll write you such a glowing review that the governor, the mayor and your captain will give you a medal. And I'll put SterlingWear on every man in the west."

He simply glared at her, then turned back to the water.

"What's the matter, Ranger. Can't we put out the wildfire and do our jobs?"

Put out the wildfire? If she sat any closer to him, the river in front of them would turn into a river of fire. "It isn't a matter of can't, Ms. McCade, it's a matter of choice. I'm not sure I like your love-'em-and-leave-'em attitude toward men."

"You mean, it's all right for men but not for women?"

"I mean—" he turned and looked out over the water again "—never mind. As you said, Ms. McCade, this is a job that we both need to complete."

"Fine. But please, call me Cat."

"Why?"

Because I want to hear you say my name. "Because my name is Catherine. 'Ms. McCade' is a little formal for two people who work together."

He faced her. "I'm not convinced we can work together. You don't like men in charge and I don't like women who don't appreciate help. Oil and water."

"True. But you're not in charge and I always appreciate the men I work with. And even though we've had our problems in this area, I think we both believe in striving for truth."

He raised an eyebrow. "So tell me the truth."

"Well, you're willing to risk your career for your convictions, even if they're wrong. You don't like women who are out front with their career. I don't like men who hide behind their rules. Too much of that and, if you're not careful, you lose your edge."

He nodded. "I'm guessing that there's no danger of you suffering from that problem."

"I'm a success, or I'm getting there, if that's what you mean, and I intend to keep on being the best at what I do. All I need is for you to help me find ordinary men I can photograph."

"That's not what Szachon is paying me to do. I'm supposed to be protecting you."

Cat stood, took a few steps toward him and leaned against one of the light posts that lined the water. "Do you really think I need protection?"

"Nope. I'd say it's the men you're stalking who are in danger. And I don't think you need me to find them, either."

"No, you'll just make it easier. I'm only interested in men who aren't phony." Her voice went deep. "Men like you." She flicked an insect off her arm without looking away. "Just look at it as a regular assignment, Ranger Dane. Whatever will be, will be."

He groaned silently. "Forget it. Men like me aren't interested in being in a cheesy catalog."

"My catalog won't be cheesy. Take a chance, Ranger. You've already found out you're wrong about me. You might be wrong about the men I intend to photograph. Do something wild for once in your life. Trust me."

Wild? Until last night he'd put being wild behind him. Wild had landed him in jail where the only escape had been to join the military. Wild was being gone when his mother had died, not even attending her funeral. Self-discipline was tough but he'd learned. The order that came with being a ranger was his life now and no matter what she thought, he'd do whatever it took to make it work. Including baby-sitting Miss Independent Hotstuff. Maybe she didn't sense the danger in their becoming a team, but he did. For whatever reason, she wanted him to work with her. He'd do it, but there was no point in making it easy. He circled the post she leaned against and started walking.

"Please, Jesse," Cat said softly as she fell in beside him, carefully avoiding any touching. "If I'm going to have a bodyguard, I need a man I won't have to fend off. One who can take me like I am and let me go when we're done. One who can help me convince the men that what I do is my job and I take it seriously."

"Look...Cat, I'm supposed to be protecting you against a threat, a threat you don't seem to be worried about at all. I don't even know what the threats are. Maybe there really is something going on. I need all the facts."

"If there is something going on, I don't know much about it, either. I'm not in the least concerned about being harmed."

"Sure. If you end up kidnapped, injured, or worse, you'll make certain that Mr. Szachon tells the mayor and the governor that I'm a real credit to the Texas Rangers," he said sarcastically. He kept walking. *Or she could be hurt and it would be his fault.*

Cat was losing him. She had to get through to him.

Finally, she hit on a way. "Look at it this way, Jesse. You can call Bettina and say, 'Nah, nah, nah' to Bettina the Matchmaker."

That brought him to a stop. "Nothing stops my sister. For the past year she's tried to match me up with one woman after another. Every woman she knows suddenly has business in San Antonio and they all have an excuse to 'look up my brother, Jesse.' I can see why Ran picked a ranch in the middle of Wyoming. At least he's harder for Bettina to get to. One of these days, we're going to join up, turn the tables and find a husband for my sister."

"In the meantime, help me do my job, Jesse."

For whatever reason, Cat McCade wanted him by her side, at least temporarily. All the time he was telling himself that he should go, he only had to think about last night and know he was going to say yes. The woman liked sex and she gave as much as she took. If ever a woman appealed to him on a primal level, this one did, and Bettina must have known that would be the case.

So he'd do his job and he'd take what was being offered for as long as Cat was in town. There was a built-in deadline with a get-out clause. And everyone involved had given him permission. But first, he'd stop by the nearest fire station and borrow a fireproof vest.

He turned to face her. "I protect you as you search

for men—strictly business. I follow your orders, and on the off chance that you are in danger, you follow mine?''

''Absolutely.''

''All right, Ms. McCade—Cat—I'll do it. When do we begin?''

''Never put off until tomorrow what you can begin tonight. If you were going babe-watching, where would you go?''

''Well, this is Texas, I'd go to the Corral.''

''Fine. What do women who go to the Corral wear?''

He eyed his shirt on her and let himself grin. ''A lot less than you are,'' he said, remembering from last night what was beneath that shirt. ''Men like long legs, long hair and—well, you get the picture.''

''I get the picture,'' she said, thinking about her wardrobe. When she'd packed, she'd thought about Texas and ranches and cows, models who were men of the land. She knew she hadn't brought the kind of outfit his grin suggested. She'd have to depend on the shopkeeper in the boutique near the hotel. She had the feeling that Sterling Szachon had high expectations of his women associates. She might only be an employee, but that wouldn't matter to him. Besides, to attract the men who would wear SterlingWear, she'd have to dress sexily.

As for Jesse James Dane, he worked hard at *not* being

one of those sexual men. The original Jesse James had been an outlaw. Maybe underneath it all, her Jesse was just as wild. She recalled the wild sex they'd shared and remembered an old expression she'd heard about being rode hard and put up wet. Water was becoming a necessary part of their relationship. All she had to do was to get within three feet of him and she needed a cold shower. Doing her job and keeping her wits about her was going to be difficult. She just wished there was a way to put Jesse on every page, because then she wouldn't need another model.

OVER HER PROTESTS, Jesse followed Cat into the boutique, and leaned back against the doorway with a toothpick in his mouth as if he were paying no attention to her actions. The salesclerk took one look at him and hurried to Cat's side.

"What can I help you with, hon?"

"I'm new in Texas," Cat said, "and I'm looking for men."

The clerk gave Jesse a long look. "You sure? I seriously doubt you'd find more than a handful of men in San Antonio that would come close to measuring up to what you've already got."

Jesse grinned. "Oh, I'm just her paid companion. I'm not even in the running. Fix her up with something that will turn heads over at the Corral."

The woman glanced at Jesse and back again. "Well, you've headed for the right place and I'd say you have the equipment for the search. I'd suggest this," the clerk said, pulling out a red dress with a short swishy skirt and a tight, low-cut top with skinny straps.

"Well, red is good, but I don't know." Cat turned her back to Jesse, glanced at the price tag and gasped. "Don't you have something with a little more dress and a little less price?"

"Honey, have you been to the Corral before?"

"No. But with a name like the Corral, I would have thought people would dress Western Style. You know, jeans...boots."

"It's as Western as money can buy. But they aren't buying denim."

"Can ordinary cowboys afford it?"

Jesse tossed the toothpick and walked over to the dress rack. He lifted the hanger holding the skimpy dress and smiled. "There *are* no ordinary cowboys in Texas. There are those who drill oil, those who raise cattle and those who become president. All of them go to the Corral whether they can afford it or not."

He reached behind her, his hand brushing her hair. There was an audible sizzle, like the feeling of nylon stockings on nylon carpet.

"What are you doing? I thought we—"

He was holding a white Stetson with a rhinestone

band. "With a dress like that, you need a hat and a pair of boots. You already have the attitude."

JESSE CARRIED the packages and escorted Cat to her room where he checked the locks, the door and the window. James Bond couldn't have done a more thorough job of making sure the room was safe.

"I'm going back to talk to Szachon," he said. "I don't like it, but if you're my job, I need to find out about this threat I'm protecting you from. What time do you want to go man hunting?"

"What time does San Antonio come alive?"

"Ask a cowboy and he'll tell you nine o'clock. Ask a Texas Ranger and he'll say the city never sleeps."

Cat gave Jesse a head-to-toe examination. She'd seen him as a dangerous man in black. She'd seen him as a spit-shiny Texas Ranger. And she'd seen him wicked and nude. She wondered which one she'd be escorted by tonight. If she had a choice, she'd forget the assignment and the clothes.

JESSE KNOCKED on Szachon's office door and waited for the invitation to enter. This time the money man was dressed in jeans and a shirt and tie. Sitting behind his desk, his expression said this was all business.

"Come in, Ranger Dane. Have a seat. I assume you've reconsidered and want to talk about the situation."

"Yes, sir." Jesse took the seat closest to the desk. "How serious is it?"

"In case you think these threats are some kind of put-up job, they aren't. Take a look at this." He handed Jesse a note, noticed his reluctance and added, "It's all right. The police have already tested it for prints. There were none."

Jesse took the folded slip of expensive linen note paper and opened it.

You think you are in charge of the *world*, Szachon.
You aren't.
I bought a knife and a gun.
Don't make me use them.

The note was written with a red marker.

"I'd think a man like you would be accustomed to this kind of thing."

"Oh, I am. Threatening me is one thing. Threatening the people I care about is another. I have a premier security force that follows through on anything that might be suspicious. Frankly, I paid no attention to it—until the tires on Elizabeth's automobile were slashed in the garage of my own hotel. With a knife."

"Tell me about Elizabeth. Is she someone close to you?" At Sterling's nod, Jesse went on. "Why don't you make a list of all your significant others—present and past. One from your past might be trying to eliminate the one in your present."

"There is no present one. Currently, I'm unattached." Those words hit Jesse hard. Szachon was looking and Cat was available.

"What about Elizabeth?"

Szachon gave a light laugh. "Elizabeth? I suppose it might be natural for an outsider to assume Elizabeth is my companion. But she's my sister."

"Tell me about her."

"Elizabeth attended design school in France and worked there for a number of years before she met and married a man I didn't approve of. Three months ago she called and said she thought her husband was having an affair. I went to London and brought her back here to stay with me. It soon became apparent that she needed something to do. This business was already on the drawing board. Now it will be hers. I don't want anything to happen to her."

"And you think the danger is real?"

Szachon shook his head. "I don't know. These threats may be nothing. I didn't think much about them until a threatening note was sent to the owner of the company manufacturing our bodywear, Daisy's Designs. Now there's Ms. McCade."

"So, what does this have to do with Ms. McCade?"

"This note came next." He pushed another sheet across the desk.

Be very careful, Zon. And believe me when I say I'm serious. Watch *all* your women. Your sister is only the first.

"So, Ranger Dane, you can see why you're here. The stalker knows Elizabeth is my sister but the threats have spread to Daisy and now Ms. McCade."

"I understand, but why hire me? You have a security firm and a police department at your command."

Szachon smiled. "Actually, I can keep Elizabeth and Daisy covered, but Ms. McCade is going to be out in public. When I mentioned my problem to the mayor he said he'd look into the threats and send his best ranger to protect my new photographer. He insisted on providing a bodyguard. I believe that he wants a man on the inside."

His best man? Yeah. "Of course, sir," Jesse said. "But Ms. McCade isn't making that easy. She seems to think she can handle anything."

Szachon smiled. "Then you're going to have a challenge, aren't you? But your captain assures me that a Texas Ranger always rises to the occasion."

That's what Jesse was afraid of.

SOMETIME after Jesse had left to announce their new working arrangement to Szachon, Cat noticed that the message light on her hotel room phone was blinking. When she pushed the proper buttons, she heard her employer's voice.

"There's a small party this evening at the Riverside Club. I wondered if you and Ranger Dane would care to join Elizabeth and me? I'd like you to get to know her. My sister has no friends in San Antonio and she seems...a bit lonely."

Cat groaned. Mr. Szachon didn't seem to realize this was business for her, not entertainment. "Thank you," was her recorded reply, "but to get the feel of the area, Ranger Dane and I plan to scout the prospects over at the Corral. Maybe another time."

Cat checked her equipment and retrieved the small Polaroid camera she intended to use for the evening. At this stage, locating prospects was simply a matter of a snapshot, a name and phone number. She'd get through the night, but beginning tomorrow, she'd take a much less public approach to her work. Real men, the kind women fantasized about, didn't often come through modeling agencies. And dressed-up peacocks on the prowl weren't her cup of tea—or, since she was in the West, weren't her cup of sarsaparilla.

Texas was virgin territory to Cat and she'd have to spend some time doing a general roundup of locations. For that, she needed to research the area. Research would take her mind off Jesse James Dane.

The tourist racks in the lobby provided brochures of sites and the gift shop had a small selection of books about the history of the state. One thing was clear, everything in the Lone Star State was more exciting, more appealing. Just plain *more*.

By midafternoon she was exhausted, not from reading but because Jesse intruded in every site she researched. He was the kind of man who might have made a stand at the Alamo, ridden with Goodnight when he drove his cattle north, fought the Comanche and drilled for oil. This had to stop. Jesse James Dane was only a man she'd slept with once. And for the next few weeks, there relationship was strictly business.

Sure it was.

FINALLY, she ran a hot bath and studied the goodie basket on her counter. It was filled with every cream and cosmetic known to women. She selected a shampoo, then creams and moisturizers. She hadn't taken this much time with her appearance since—ever. She dried her hair, allowing it to fall straight to her shoulders. Bare-legged was the way to go, she decided as she donned boots and the dress. When she turned to look at herself in the mirror she blinked and closed her eyes. She was fulfilling the ranger's prophesy. Everything about her said "I'm hot and I'm looking."

But she wasn't. This wasn't her. The only men she

was looking for were normal guys who, through the magic of her camera, would turn into every woman's greatest fantasy. Dressed like this, she realized that the kind of man she'd attract was the kind of man she avoided. Just as she reached for the zipper in the back of her dress to slide it down, there was a knock at her door.

"Just a minute. I'm coming." But the zipper wouldn't go down and it wouldn't go up. The knock became more insistent. If this was the way the evening was going, she might as well end it right now. Frustrated, she unlocked the door and jerked it open. "I said I was coming."

"Without me?"

5

CAT LET OUT a deep breath. "I don't think so."

Ranger Jesse James Dane filled her doorway and she suddenly felt as if all the air had been sucked out of the room. He was wearing black jeans, boots with silver toes and a gray shirt that made his eyes look like glazed granite. Tonight he held a Stetson as black as his hair. His face and chin were roughened with day-old stubble and he smelled like the sage she'd inhaled in his shirt.

"Oh," she said, giving the word at least three extra breathless oh's. Her arms were crossed at her chest, holding the dress. "I put on the dress you and the woman in the dress shop..." Her voice trailed off and she added, "But it isn't me. I decided to change but I can't get the zipper to..." She was babbling. Every instinct she possessed told her that she ought to close the door, get into the El Camino and head back to Atlanta. But she couldn't move. She knew he felt it, too, for he shook his head slowly and took a step forward, studying her crossed arms.

"Need some help?"

"No. I mean, yes." Closing her eyes, she turned around.

She heard retreating footsteps, then a click.

"You locked the door?"

"I did. And I expect you to keep it locked." His voice grew closer again. "I talked to Szachon and I've had second thoughts about our going out this evening. You might be in danger."

"You can't be serious. Why would anyone threaten to harm me?"

"I have no idea. But now that I've seen you in that dress, I'd rather you stay put until I have time to do some investigating."

Cat bristled. "No way, Ranger. Nobody tells me where I can go. I have a job to do. But you're right. I'm not wearing this." She gave the zipper a final tug and swore. "Get me out of it, please."

Jesse hoped his expression didn't show that getting her out of the dress would be exactly what he'd do if he had the choice. As for accompanying her on a manhunt, he supposed he'd have to go. She obviously wouldn't be stopped. With a sigh, he tossed his hat onto a table, came to her side and reached out, hesitating inches from her left breast as she lifted her arm. He swallowed hard and caught the sides of the top of the dress, pulling them together so that he could force the placket up, then down, leaving her back exposed. "Okay."

She walked away, his fingertips tingling as though he'd actually touched her naked breasts. She was making her statement. Catherine McCade was her own woman. And he liked that. Too much.

In less than five minutes Cat returned. She was still wearing the boots, but the red dress had been replaced by a pair of leather pants and a tank top with Look, But Don't Touch spelled out across the front in red glitter.

"'Look, but don't touch?' I hope you know what you're doing, Cat McCade. I'm not sure these Texas boys read."

"Then I expect you to read it for them," she said, picking up her Stetson and heading for the door. "You're my bodyguard, Ranger Dane, so guard my body."

"Aren't you taking your camera?" he asked, planting his own Stetson on his head and following her.

"Of course," she said, dropping the small camera into her shoulder purse. "A photographer never goes anywhere without it."

Look, but don't touch. He'd been telling himself that for the past twelve hours. He had every intention of following his own orders. It was a mental thing and he prided himself on his ability to focus. But every time he touched Cat, his stern resolve melted away. He might

be the first bodyguard in history to hire a bodyguard to
protect a body from the guard.

THE CORRAL WAS ALIVE. The lineup for admission was
already long.

"Popular place," Cat said. "I didn't realize there
would be such a crowd."

"Oh, yes. You wanted cowboys, you got cowboys."
Jesse took her elbow and guided her to the door. "Yo,
Bull."

The man standing guard was as big as a bull and just
as wicked-looking. At the sound of Jesse's voice, he
looked up, caught sight of him and broke into a big
grin. "Hello, man. What brings you to my part of
town?" Then he caught sight of Cat and gave a long
whistle. "Never mind. I can see what brought you
here, but if it was me, I'd take this lady away from all
these yahoos and keep her all to myself."

"Bull, this is Ms. Cat McCade and she wants to check
out those yahoos," Cat said.

Bull grinned. "Okay, but don't say I didn't warn
you. Tie up your horse and come on in." He stepped
aside, making room for Cat and Jesse to enter.

The bodies quickly closed in, forcing Jesse against
Cat. They had little choice except to move with the
crowd. The music was loud, the beat accompanied by
the simultaneous clatter of boot heels. It didn't take Cat

long to realize two things. One, what looked like a series of simple moves, wasn't. And two, not a cowboy there could compare with Jesse James Dane. She could have added a third. Rhinestones were a phenomenal conductor of heat.

The band stopped playing. The dancers gave a "Yehaw!" and used another comment as they left the floor that caused Cat's eyes to widen. Some headed back to their tables and others to the bar.

"See anybody you like?" Jesse asked.

"Not yet. We need to circulate and get a feel for the place. But this crowd is going to make that hard."

"You don't know how right you are," Jesse muttered under his breath, trying to stay a decent distance from her in a mass of humanity intent on pushing them together.

She gave a quick look over her shoulder and shouted, "When I said get the feel for the place, I didn't mean I had to feel every person in the bar!"

He leaned over to speak in her ear. "Why not? A good photographer uses whatever comes her way, doesn't she?"

She stopped dead-still, remembering that he'd said she'd have to shoot the catalog without his help, then she pressed back against him and grinned. "You're right, Ranger. Time to go to work." She pulled off her Stetson and handed it to him, then, taking out her camera, she made her way to the bar, studying the men leaned against it as if they were sides of beef being auditioned for a barbecue.

Jesse wasn't comfortable with her move but he had no choice but to stand back and let her do her thing. Just as long as she stayed close enough so that he could intervene if necessary.

Finally she stopped and flipped her hair over her shoulder while she focused her camera on one particular patron. "Hi, cowboy, would you let me photograph you?"

"Why sure, darlin', but why settle for a picture when you can have the real thing?"

"You don't understand," Cat said. "I'm looking for special men and once I find them, *then* I take them home. Right now, you're just running in the herd. Why don't you jump up on the bar and show me your best stuff?"

Her subject reached out, caught Cat by the waist and swung her onto the bar, then vaulted up behind her. "Sure, you and me. Let's show these yahoos a thing or two."

Jesse didn't waste any time stepping up. Fun was fun, but he'd noticed the crowd was getting into the game—and that could be dangerous. Time for him to earn his money. "Look but don't touch," Jesse said. "You see her message, don't you?" He held up his arms for Cat, who ignored them. Instead she sat on the bar and then slid off it to stand on the floor. The guy on the bar jumped down beside her.

"Cheese it, Durango," Bull growled from behind, "you're crossing a Texas Ranger."

"That right?" the guy beside Cat asked.

Jesse nodded.

Immediately, the bar stools emptied and the subject of Cat's photo shoot disappeared into the crowd, taking most of the onlookers with him.

"Thanks, Jesse," Cat snapped. "Did I ask you to interfere?"

"Didn't have to. I'm being paid to protect you."

"And I'm being paid for a job and I don't intend to let you mess that up. We might as well go."

She whirled around and, with Jesse behind her, headed toward the dance area where the men and women were lined up like gunfighters at a showdown. Cat marched down the center, the lights reflecting off the rhinestone studs on the front of her shirt like star bursts. If she'd been a steer she'd be snorting steam.

Jesse decided a little punishment for Cat and pleasure for the customers was in order. He looked at the crowd and grinned. "No way, lady. Nobody comes to the Corral without dancing. It's a Texas tradition, isn't it, boys?" He caught her camera and stuck it back into her purse, fitted her Stetson back on her head then wedged her into line opposite him.

"Even a Texas Ranger can have a little fun with his lady, can't he?"

"Yee-haw!" the band leader called as he dragged his bow across the strings of his fiddle.

"I'm not your lady and I don't know how to do this," she protested.

"I'll teach you."

Though the steps were intricate, it didn't seem to matter if she didn't know what she was doing. And it was obvious that the dancers took Jesse's claim to heart. She was his woman and they handled her with kid gloves, touching her as little and as politely as possible. She wasn't going to find any candidates here, now that he'd put his brand on her. And he was right about his move—she needed to make peace with the patrons by joining in on the fun.

In no time she'd let go of her concern and was stomping her boots with the best of them. It didn't take her long to realize that she was being taught by a master. It took even less time for Cat to see that the women were very interested in Jesse. The eyes of Texas, at least the female eyes, were definitely on him. And they were undressing him with those eyes. If she had a sample case filled with SterlingWear, and Jesse James Dane modeling it, she'd sell out in a few minutes.

Then the music changed and the dancers split into couples. Cat moved naturally into Jesse's arms, and his hand against her back guided her around the floor in a brisk step that soon had her breathless. Her body felt as if every nerve ending had fired, each movement giving a fresh jolt.

"Nice going, Cat," he said, giving her a wicked smile. "I'm surprised that you're into the two-step."

"I'm a quick learner," she replied, lifting herself to speak into his ear. She caught a whiff of the same sage she'd smelled on his shirt. "After all, a woman like me has to learn how to please all kinds of men." She returned his wicked grin and took a deliberate short step that brought his body against hers.

Suddenly the lightness went out of the moment.

"You're playing with fire, Cat McCade," Jesse said.

"So I am." She grew more serious. "That's something I don't usually do. And I don't think you do, either. If I get too crazy, you have my permission to call me on it."

"I'll tell you what I think—it's time to get out of here," he said roughly. Then he turned and took her hand, pulling her through the crowd along the side of the dance area.

"You leaving?" Bull asked. He took another look at Cat and added, "Don't blame you. I'm thinking about leaving, too. This job is too undignified for a man of my gentle nature." He gave Cat a wink. "If he doesn't show you a good time, darlin', you just let me know."

She smiled with amusement and kept moving through the onlookers, closing her ears to the comments of the cowboys who made similar offers. When they reached the sidewalk, she turned away from the sound of the music, expecting Jesse to let go of her hand. He didn't. Instead he stopped her for a moment and looked carefully down the walk ahead, then swung around and studied the walkers behind.

"Are you looking for somebody?" she asked.

"I'm being paid to protect you, remember?"

She laughed. "I'm sorry. I don't believe for one minute that I'm in danger. I've been surrounded by angry music fans, by advertisers and, once, by a tribe of African natives who didn't approve of having their photographs taken. This whole thing is some kind of put-on."

"I thought you just photographed men."

"When I started, I was a photographer's assistant. I went where the boss went and that took me to some weird places."

Jesse couldn't say he had the kind of strong feeling of danger that came when something was wrong. Something didn't ring true, and Jesse planned to get to the bottom of it. In fact, he'd made a telephone call before he'd picked up Cat that had set the wheels in motion back at headquarters. They'd check out Szachon's business competition, his enemies and his ex-companions. "We can't assume the notes are fake. On the off chance there is someone out there who wants to make trouble, I have to protect you."

Cat kept pace with Jesse's long, slow stride. Their hips touched occasionally when they passed other walkers along the river. A flat-bottomed boat moved slowly down the water, carrying a small table where a candlelight dinner was being served to a couple. Jesse liked that Cat seemed content to stroll without talking. It was comfortable. But there was one thing he had to do. He owed her an apology and that was not going to be easy for him.

"I'm sorry I misjudged you, Cat," he finally said. "You're a beautiful woman. When you said men were your business and you were going to meet a prospective employer at the Palace. I just jumped to the wrong conclusions."

"Is this an apology?"

"No. I mean... Yes! Hell! I don't know what I mean." She was doing it again, making him lose control. "Let's start again, Cat McCade. I'm sorry I thought you were a hooker. One thing you learn in law enforcement is not to judge a person. I did. I won't do that again." He glanced at her. "But in order not to do that, I need to know more."

"So, what do you want to know?"

"For starters, how'd you get into bikes and antique cars?"

"That's going to help you protect me?"

"No, that's going to tell me why I like you."

A surprised "oh" was her immediate response. She hadn't expected that. And she didn't know how to deal with it. He liked her? Quickly she went into the kind of gibberish he evoked. "My dad wanted a boy. He had three girls. I learned early on that if I wanted any approval from him, I had to find a way to please him. And it wasn't going to be easy to fake an interest in cooking and dancing lessons. He liked restoring classic cars and I found out I had him to myself then. And I did like being the only girl on base with a motorcycle."

"On base? That's right. Your father was a colonel in the army."

"That's another reason I've seen so much of the world."

"And why you're so independent, I'd guess. I should have recognized the symptoms."

"What symptoms?"

He was about to answer, to explain he was an ex-marine, when a woman's scream cut through the sounds of the River Walk.

Jesse hesitated, reluctant to leave Cat's side, then told her to stay put with two other women who'd also stopped. Then he headed quickly toward the sprawling cypress tree ahead. He ducked around the trunk to find a man trying to rip a purse from a woman's hands. When the thief saw Jesse, he let go, knocked the woman to the ground and headed around the back of the tree—where Cat was set to tackle him.

Jesse stopped up short as Cat dove for the thief, bounced off him and into the canal. As the thief scrambled off, a backward glance told Jesse that a passerby had pulled the frightened victim to her feet. Jesse turned back to Cat who, waist-deep in the river, spit water as she headed toward the bank.

"Sorry, can't give you more than a six on that," he said, and held out his hand.

She grinned, jerked her arm and sent him flying into the four-foot-deep canal. "That's better than your five," she said, sputtering. "Was the woman hurt?"

"No," Jesse answered, vaulting out of the water. This time he simply stood and let Cat get out on her own. "A mugger, apparently. But when he saw me, he let go of the woman's purse and ran. Are you okay?"

Cat picked up her own purse from where she'd dropped it on the bank, then draped it over her shoulder. Someone handed her the Stetson she'd lost and she crammed it back onto her head. "I told you I can take care of myself. I know kickboxing and I'm a very good swimmer. I even know how to fire a weapon."

She shivered visibly. "Now, I'm going back to the hotel. If you want to come along, I'll try to protect you."

The squish of Cat's boots reminded him of how foolish he must look to the cowboys who'd followed them outside the Corral and milled around.

When they reached the Palace lobby, Cat tried to dismiss Jesse with a curt, "Thank you for accompanying me, Ranger Dane, but I can get to my room without any help."

"I don't doubt that for a moment, but I'm coming with you anyway."

Ignoring the amused looks of the guests and employees, Cat and Jesse, still dripping, made their way to the elevator and to the penthouse floor. Jesse insisted on entering the room first. He switched on the light and let out a low whistle. "Oh, boy!"

The room had been destroyed. An alcoholic looking for his last bottle couldn't have done a better job of ransacking. Her films had all been exposed; her camera cases slashed and her clothes tossed everywhere.

Cat stepped into the middle of the room and looked around in shock. "Who'd do such a thing?" she whispered.

Jesse walked around the room, studying the scene closer. "Somebody who wants you to know you're not welcome."

Cat switched on the light in the bathroom. "Jesse, look at this."

On the mirror, Watch Out. You're Next! was written in dark red lipstick.

"Son of a..." She picked up a towel to wipe away the message but Jesse stopped her. "Coward!" she shouted instead. There was a catch in her voice that sounded like a sob.

Jesse reached out and pulled her into his arms. "Nobody's going to harm you. You have a bodyguard. Remember?"

"I'm not afraid. I'm mad!" She pounded his chest with her fists. "Nobody is going to mess this up for me. Nobody!"

He led her back to the main room and caught her hands and held them for a moment, looking into her eyes. "I'll call the captain and Szachon. You look around here to see if anything has been stolen."

She pulled away, strolled around, then picked up her favorite camera and frowned. "The carrying case for this one is gone. Why would anybody break in, ransack the place, and take the case and not the camera? That makes no sense."

"None of this makes sense. Don't touch anything else. We need to check for fingerprints." He went to the phone and asked to be put through to Szachon's private phone. Moments later he was talking in a low tone. "Yes, sir. She's going to need to be moved while I arrange for this room to be checked out."

After he informed Captain Wade, Cat was whisked downstairs to a suite on a lower floor. The head of hotel security met Jesse and Cat there. He opened the door and moved inside where he checked the room.

"List the occupant of this room as Hazel Smith," Jesse said, taking the key.

"Hazel Smith?" Cat let out a chortle. She didn't know whether it was amusement or shock. "Is that the best you can do?"

"Sorry, it was the first thing that came to mind. Szachon is sending his sister down. You've seen her picture, right? She's bringing you some dry clothes and she'll stay with you. Make sure it's Elizabeth before you open the door."

"I don't need a baby-sitter, Jesse."

"No, but Elizabeth might."

6

NOTHING about what had happened made sense to Jesse, except he'd let the woman he was supposed to be protecting end up in the river. Simple task. Keep her safe. He hadn't. Self-recrimination swept over him, leaving him momentarily stunned. Granted, she hadn't been hurt, but she could have been. He'd been willing to dismiss the mugging as coincidence. But now that he'd seen Cat's room, he realized that someone was letting him know that she could be gotten to. The question was, who?

And he was angry, not at Cat but at himself. He'd been hired to protect her and twice he'd let himself get distracted. Certainly he couldn't ignore a woman's cry for help, but in coming to the stranger's aid, he'd left his charge. And now he couldn't even be certain that the incident had been on the level. The mugger had escaped and the woman had vanished. And Cat— He didn't even want to think about allowing her to be hurt.

The local crime scene investigators arrived in Cat's room within minutes. A murder scene couldn't have been more carefully examined. The black dust left by the fingerprint experts added to the chaos. In the end, they determined that the door hadn't been jimmied and only the camera case was missing. It was as if a mischievous child had thrown a tantrum in Cat's room and made a mess. Except for the message on the mirror. That was personal.

"What's going on, Dane?" Sterling Szachon appeared, his tone a resounding indication of his displeasure.

"It seems that someone wants Ms. McCade to know she isn't welcome."

"A fact I thought we were both aware of. What happened? I was told she was attacked and thrown into the river."

"Not exactly. There was a mugging. When I went to help the woman, her attacker dropped the purse and ran. Wonder Woman here tried to tackle him and ended up in the canal. I thought at the time it was an honest—" he gave a dry laugh "—mugging. Now I'm not sure. It could have been a diversion so that we wouldn't return to her room too soon. But I think it's another warning. Take a look at the bathroom mirror. Whoever is behind these threats is going public."

Szachon strode to the bathroom, looked at the message on the mirror and swore. He turned back to his security chief. "How'd they get in?"

"We're trying to figure that out, sir. We don't have the results of the fingerprint checks, but for now it seems to be an inside job."

"You mean, someone managed to get onto this floor and into this room?"

"The cameras?" Jesse asked.

"Turned off," the chief said.

"I don't like this," Szachon snapped.

"I want the service elevator taken out of service. Post someone at the elevator on this floor and downstairs," Jesse said.

"Agreed."

When the security director realized that Jesse was in charge, he nodded and added, "And in the morning, all the locking codes will be changed. In the meantime, we're checking on all personnel with access to this floor."

Szachon walked over to Jesse. "Protecting Ms. Mc-Cade is your job, Ranger. Any thoughts on this?"

"I don't have anything to add yet. But I agree with your security chief that it's likely an inside job. And if whoever did it was serious, Cat's equipment would have been destroyed. I still think this is some kind of warning. Maybe the men of Texas don't want to buy your underwear."

"Or maybe they don't want Elizabeth to run the company," Szachon said thoughtfully. "Where is Elizabeth?"

Jesse answered. "I thought it best to remove Ms. McCade from the floor until we got a handle on what happened. Your sister is with her in a suite down on fifteen. I didn't want to alarm her so I just told her that your photographer needed some dry clothing and some company."

Szachon nodded and looked at his security chief. "You're posting a guard on the suite for the evening?"

"Not necessary," Jesse said. "You just watch Elizabeth and Daisy. I'll be in Ms. McCade's room for the night and there'll be a man on the elevator. That's enough."

"Looks like you need some dry clothes," the security guard observed. "Want me to watch the ladies while you get some?"

"I'll be fine," Jesse snapped. He'd already left Cat once and she'd ended up in the river. He turned to one of the technicians. "Go over the room again. Check every inch for prints. I'll talk to you in the morning."

He barked the order but he knew they'd find nothing except the prints of people who could have been in the room legitimately. He was being toyed with and he didn't like that.

At least his boots didn't squish anymore as he stepped on the elevator.

CAT DIDN'T KNOW if Elizabeth's agitation was from fear or just plain nerves. Followed by a hotel security guard, she'd appeared at Cat's door with an escort and identified herself as Sterling's sister.

"I was told to bring you some dry clothes and these SterlingWear samples. What happened to you?"

"Somebody pushed me into the river."

"Oh, dear. You could have drowned."

"Not in four feet of water. Besides, it was an accident. There was a mugger who ran into me as he tried to get away."

"But why did they move you from your room?" Elizabeth asked.

"When we got back to the hotel, we discovered that someone had broken in. Whoever it was destroyed all my film and took one of my camera bags."

Elizabeth looked puzzled. "Destroyed your film? Had you taken some kind of pictures that you shouldn't have?"

"Not likely. I haven't photographed anything yet. But that wasn't the worst thing. My burglar left a threatening message on the bathroom mirror."

"I'm worried, Ms. McCade," Elizabeth said. "Maybe Zon needs to give up this idea about SterlingWear. It isn't worth having anyone get hurt."

"You know your brother better than I do, but he doesn't strike me as the kind of man who'd be intimidated."

"He's like my husband. Nobody intimidates him, either. Neither of them ever tolerates anyone disagreeing with them. They certainly don't listen to me."

There was an odd tone in Elizabeth's voice. Cat didn't know how to respond. Zon had set up this business so that Elizabeth would have something to do, and she had been trained in fashion, so Cat couldn't see the problem. "Are you worried about Sterling-Wear?" Cat asked.

"No. I'm sure it will be a success. Everything Zon touches turns to gold. And I can run the business, if he'll let me. I just—" She cut off her sentence and shook her head. "Don't mind me. I'm just being emotional. This is the first business I've ever headed up and this is my first divorce."

The next visitor was a member of the security staff delivering hot water, tea bags, coffee and pastries. "Mr. Szachon thought you might enjoy a snack, Ms. McCade, and you, too, Mrs. Vadin."

Cat gave him a smile and a nod. "Thank you."

Elizabeth paid no attention. She went to the window, looked out, then came back to the cart. Cat felt as if she were caught in the middle of something she didn't understand. Maybe Elizabeth was more worried than she wanted to admit.

"Let's have some of that coffee," Cat suggested, reaching for the thermal pot.

"No, I think I'll have tea," Elizabeth countered. "I've been in England so long that I've adopted their preferences. You see, the staff included clotted cream and scones."

She poured Cat's coffee then ripped open a paper packet, removed the tea bag, dropped it into a cup and covered it with hot water.

Cat added artificial sweetener and cream to her coffee. "I notice you have an accent. How long have you lived in England?"

"Most of my life, except for the time I spent in school in Paris."

"But Mr. Szachon seems totally American."

"Sterling and I share the same mother," Elizabeth explained, taking a seat in the quiet room. "But his father is a Texas rancher. My father is an English duke. No great wealth attached to the title now, but my mother fancied living abroad."

"What happened to your parents?" Cat asked as she plopped into the chair opposite Elizabeth.

"They were killed in a skiing accident when I was seventeen. Sterling became my guardian, a job he still takes very seriously."

Cat couldn't control the look of puzzlement on her face. "But you're married, aren't you?"

"Yes." There was a long silence before she added, "For now."

Elizabeth sprang to her feet and walked back to the window overlooking the River Walk. She stood for a moment, then shrugged her shoulders, turned and smiled. "Don't listen to me," she said. "I do like the idea of having my own business. I've had a brother and a husband telling me what to do all my life. Now, I'm going to find out if I can do it myself. After all, I was trained for this."

"What kind of training?"

"I studied fashion at the Institute of Design and Art at the Sorbonne. Then I met Raoul. He was wealthy, talented. So full of ambition and determination. I fell in love with him over a weekend and we married the next month.

"I didn't know it then, but I'd married a man as controlling as my brother." She jutted out her chin and added, "That's all over now. He never believed that I would do it, but I've left him."

"Sometimes divorce is the best answer," Cat murmured.

"You're right. It's just that divorce is so final. I hadn't thought my life would change so drastically. I didn't think he'd let me leave. I believed I'd be married forever."

"Forever can be a different kind of problem," Cat

said, thinking of her mother. "I mean, my mother and father have been married for almost fifty years."

"And he still loves her?"

Cat gave a dry laugh. "That's hard to tell. To him love and responsibility is the same thing. My father isn't a touchy-feely kind of man and he has very high expectations of all his family. But, to his credit, he'd defend us to the end."

Like Jesse, she thought. But she was beginning to believe that Jesse liked her and she was never sure about her father. "Do you think somebody is really threatening us?"

Elizabeth returned to the cart and pinched off a corner of one of the pastries, then held it as if she'd forgotten why she'd done so. "Yes. Why wouldn't I?"

Cat decided that Elizabeth was the kind of woman depicted in fairy tales: slim, red-haired, almost ethereal in her beauty. She couldn't imagine any man divorcing such a beauty, especially when she was the half sister of one of the richest men in the world. "If your husband is a mover and shaker like Mr. Szachon, your family must have amassed incredible power."

"My husband hated my brother, hated that Zon had more money, could move in circles Raoul couldn't. I think when he found out who I was, he married me thinking I would raise his social position. He never believed that I personally didn't care about money and status. And he would never let me help him. I was his woman and I was to be taken care of—"

At an abrupt knock on the door, Cat rose and Elizabeth froze.

Thankfully, the new arrival was Ranger Jesse James Dane. Once he'd entered, Elizabeth dropped the pastry and insisted on returning to her own quarters. Despite Jesse's assurances that she would be better off staying with Cat for the night, Elizabeth overruled him. There was little for Jesse to do other than let the guard outside the door escort her to her room.

"Don't let her out of your sight," Jesse said as he watched them leave. "Make sure she has a guard. And get back down here when she's safe." When they stepped into the elevator, Jesse closed Cat's door and locked it.

Cat looked at Jesse and shivered. She picked up the clothes Elizabeth had brought and headed for the bedroom.

"I don't know what you're going to do about your clothes but you might look inside that bag. There might be something useful to you. It contains SterlingWear samples." Cat ran her hand through her blond strands. "I'm going to wash that river water out of my hair." Then she diverted a look at Jesse.

"Once I'm clean and dry, I want more of that coffee and some answers."

Jesse raised an eyebrow. "Do I salute or will 'Yes, ma'am' be enough?"

CAT LET THE HOT WATER sluice over her, removing the grit from her hair and the tension from her body. What had she gotten herself into? A contract to shoot the catalog for SterlingWear was not only a feather in her cap but a welcome addition to her dangerously low bank account. Yes she'd done well. Yes she had a name. But the instability of the economy in the past year had made her realize that her future was less secure than she might have liked.

She felt a wave of guilt. Poor Elizabeth was about to start a career that would certainly make her secure, but she was losing the husband she obviously still loved. Life was a trade-off. But opportunities Cat had always taken for granted might not always be there for her, either. What would it be like to team up with a man, to plan a future that tied you to him, and then lose him?

That thought made her shiver, even under the hot water. Her mother had done that. She hadn't actually lost her husband; he simply spent all his time playing golf and tennis with his military buddies, leaving her mother with nothing to do. She had to be lonely. Or was she?

Maybe Cat's assumption that she knew what was best for her own mother was just like Elizabeth's husband knowing what was best for her…. Cat gave a little sigh. She had to admit that her sisters seemed happy. And they swore that their mother was, as well. Cat didn't understand her mother. She understood her father better. But the truth was, she didn't like him very much. She'd failed both parents' expectations, choosing to make her own way.

It was just that, sometimes *she* was lonely. Recently she hadn't spent time with any of her male models. That had to be the reason her one-night stand with Jesse had been so explosive. And now the man who'd lit the fuse was waiting in the parlor of her hotel suite.

She turned off the water and stepped out, wrapping herself into the blanket-sized towel.

In the bath on the other side of the parlor, Jesse heard Cat's shower go silent. He glanced into the mirror and groaned. He hadn't shaved earlier in the evening because the grubby look had seemed to fit his bodyguard persona. But now he looked like the ax murderer he'd once warned Cat about. He tousled his wet hair, wrapped a towel around his waist and padded barefoot back into the parlor. He was on the phone with the bellman when Cat came in.

"Yes. Would you send someone up to pick up my clothes? I need them cleaned as soon as possible. Yes, I know it's midnight," he growled. "Yes, early morning will do if you can't arrange it any sooner."

"Do you think they would let me have my comb and brush from my room?" Cat asked quietly, tying the sash of the terry-cloth robe she wore.

"Not until they're through with the crime scene."

Cat laughed dryly. "Do you really think my room is a crime scene?"

"Yes," Jesse admitted. "I don't think they'll find any prints that aren't supposed to be there. But your boss can make enough noise to send heads rolling. Nobody is going to take a chance." Jesse called again and ordered a comb and brush.

Shortly after, the bellman appeared with the comb and brush and took away both Jesse's and Cat's river-soggy clothing. He'd have them back "first thing in the morning."

As the door closed, they were standing across the room from each other, their reflections in the mirror on the center wall. Jesse pretended he didn't feel the tingle at the back of his neck, didn't feel his pulse quicken. He should have taken a chair outside the suite, wet clothes or not. Now he was trapped inside a private, locked hideaway that invited disaster.

"So you think nobody is going to take a chance on angering Mr. Szachon?" Cat said, towel-drying her hair just as she had done in front of Jesse's fireplace.

"That's right. They're going to cross every *t* and dot

every *i*. The problem is that this all makes no sense. It's throwing everyone for a loop." *Including me.*

"Including us." She echoed his thoughts. "I've spoiled your normal routine, and after what you did today, you certainly spoiled mine."

"And what did I do to *spoil* your routine?"

"You became a Texas Ranger in a place where the men don't want their backgrounds investigated. Once word gets around, I'll be lucky if I can find enough prospects to choose from."

"Cat, you were one step away from causing a riot at the Corral. I'm supposed to protect you."

"I don't need you to protect me," she snapped, leaning forward so that she could layer her hair between the folds of the towel. Her movement caused the lower section of her robe to part, exposing those long legs that had kept him sleepless the night before.

"I intend to do my job, no matter what you say." His clenched muscles turned to stone and trembled from his effort to stop the invasion of heat that rippled through his body every time he was close to her. He hoped she wasn't aware of his desire. He wished his own body wasn't.

Across the room, Cat's drying motions mimicked her silent pleas. *Don't let him know what I'm feeling. Don't let me rip off that towel and throw myself on him. Don't let me attack him.*

"Jesse, this isn't going to work."

"What isn't going to work?"

"You staying here tonight."

"Why not?"

"You're half naked. I mean, I'm used to having men running around in their underwear, but that was business."

He laughed. "And this isn't?"

"We—no. I mean, we aren't selling towels. And you're not one of my models."

He filled a cup with coffee and studied her. She was visibly upset. Somehow, this woman who was so accustomed to dealing with men was having difficulty dealing with him. He sensed that this strong attraction between them was as hard for her to handle as it was for him. Something had to give before they destroyed each other. This time she wasn't going to be the one who said she wanted him.

"What was it you said you ask all your prospects to do?" he asked.

"My prospects?"

He put the carafe down and walked around the cart, toward her. "Yeah, the men who are auditioning?"

She couldn't believe what he was doing. Surely he hadn't forgotten their agreement. They'd forget what had happened, work through this project and get on with their lives. He'd get back his reputation and she'd get the kind of job that gave her long-term stability. *Stability?* Even the thought of that word hurt her brain.

"Tell me again what you'd ask them to do?" he repeated.

She tried not to think about that. She couldn't even answer. If she opened her mouth she'd say something like, "I want to sleep with you."

No, that was dishonest. What she'd say was that she wanted to tie him to the bedposts and rub against every inch of his body.

"Forget about it, Jesse. You're not one of my models. What happened before was wrong."

"Wrong isn't the word I'd use," he said, unfastened the tucked-in towel and let it fall. "Wrong is when someone doesn't measure up. You're in the business of finding men. Examine me."

"What are you doing?" she gasped.

"I'm auditioning. Well, not exactly. I'd have to wear your product, wouldn't I?" He made a move toward the bag on the couch.

"Don't do this, Jesse," she said, stopping him in his tracks.

"Why not? Accept it, Cat. No matter what we tell ourselves, we can't be inseparable and not make love. It ain't gonna happen. I can't think about my job and neither can you with this fire burning us up. The only answer I can come up with is that we put it out. I'll admit, seduction is new to me. You have a better idea?"

He was right. Her desire for him was constant, so constant that it was threatening her professional life. Being in his arms was all she thought about. She could handle this. He probably thought she'd back down. He was wrong.

Cat dropped her own towel and caught the ties of her robe. She moved closer. She didn't know where this was going but she couldn't have stopped it if she'd tried.

"What are you doing?" he asked.

She smiled and walked around him, examining him from his toes to his knees to his thighs to— "I'm inspecting the merchandise. I have to be very sure. Sometimes light and shadows, even the angle, can deceive."

"Look all you want," Jesse observed tersely. "I try hard to please."

"Oh, yes." She grinned, reached out and touched him. "'Hard' doesn't seem to be a problem, Jesse James Dane. Tell me what *you* think we're doing?"

"Damned if I know. I expected you to slap my face, flee into your bedroom and lock the door. You didn't. You're a bold woman, Catherine McCabe. And you're turning me into a bold man." Her hand rested on his shoulder, making fingerprints of heat. "As long as I'm guarding you, I can't leave and you can't go. And if you don't stop touching me, we're going to have to figure out a way to handle this or we're both going to be sorry."

"Will you really be sorry, Jesse?"

"I don't know...and I don't think I care," he said, and jerked her hand away, pulling her closer in the move. He'd admired her long legs; he just hadn't realized that they'd bring her against him in a way he wasn't prepared for. His hardness slid perfectly into the vee between them and he gasped.

"Oh!" she moaned. "Looks like your stress is looking for relief."

"Cat, I don't have any way to protect you."

"You don't need to." She shook her arms, allowing the robe to drop. She moved her hips back and forth against him.

"But you let me...I mean, you put the condom on me last night."

"I just wanted to torture you. Believe me, it's all right, Jesse, or it will be if you don't make this last all day." She tightened her arms around him and backed to the couch, pulling him along as she fell against it, spread her legs and curled them around him.

And then he was inside her. She was right. Any longer and he would have been too late. He'd always prided himself on satisfying the woman he was making love to, but Cat made love as she did everything else. She went after pleasure and embraced it. She was like a smouldering firecracker ready to go off, and every moment they spent together built the explosion higher. Foreplay was obsolete. The force of their climax rocked him with its intensity. Afterward, he thought he'd never felt so drained, so sated.

Then he came back to his senses. What in hell was he doing? With a groan, he stood and looked down at her. "Okay, we've proved my point. We can't do this," he said in a tight voice.

She smiled up at him lazily and stretched. "I know. You don't break the rules. You're a Texas Ranger and this goes against everything you stand for. You know something? It goes against all my rules, too. I like men and I like sex. But I don't want the complications of a relationship any more than you do. Still, I don't see any other answer. We can't be close to each other without setting off the fire alarms. Got any better ideas?"

Jesse picked up his towel and retied it around his waist. "Is that what this is, a relationship?"

She slowly got off the couch and pulled on her robe. "I don't know. I've tried to avoid learning anything about them. Relationships turn into roots."

"They're not for me, either. Up to now, I've made love to a woman and then I've gone home."

Cat stared at him. "You've made love and you've

gone home? Correction, you've had sex and you've gone home. Don't rangers believe in watching the sun rise with a lover?"

"Not this one, certainly not with a woman he's charged to protect."

"Speaking of protection, I take a birth control shot every six months." Her voice grew tight, holding back something that felt like anger. "So you don't have to worry about protecting me."

"I hate to tell you this, lady, but that shot won't protect you from whoever may be out to get you." This wasn't working out, Jesse realized. Everything was out of sync, except the wire of heat that held them together. Making love hadn't helped. The connection was still as strong as before. He turned and walked to the door.

She wanted to reach out and put her arms around Jesse. She liked this man. No matter what she'd told Bettina, it had been nearly a year since she'd been with one, and even then it hadn't been as it was with Jesse. It had never been the way it was with Jesse. This was different and she didn't know why. When she'd seen him charging around that cypress tree, concern in his eyes, she'd realized how her heart had cried out to know he would be all right. When he'd said he liked her, she realized she liked him, too.

Now she'd broken her own rule. This wasn't sharing sex with a willing acquaintance, this was making love to a man who was becoming very special to her. She wished she had his shirt. The shirt and its scent of sage had become her comfort.

When she looked his way, she saw that the expression on Jesse's face was hard.

She may like this man but she wasn't going to let him boss her around. "I'll be replacing my film, my camera case and my clothing first thing in the morning." She gestured toward the window. "I can see a construction site down below. I'm ready to look for men tomorrow, and you can accompany me or not. It's up to you. But you'd better not scare my models away or I'll ask for another bodyguard."

Jesse watched the door to her room close behind her with a hollow thud.

He felt charged, his energy level at an all-time high. But it wasn't his work he was thinking of. It was Cat. He had to find out who was behind the threats quick, or the controversy he'd stirred up with the dead body at the cemetery would pale in comparison to the trouble Cat would cause by asking Szachon to replace him.

This was his career, his future at risk.

Hell. It wasn't his career he was having trouble dealing with, it was lust and a too-hot-to-handle beauty who was sealed off behind a closed door. The guys back at headquarters joked that men didn't think with their brains. They could be right.

At 3:00 A.M., just after his head had hit the pillow, the phone rang. Jesse was still awake, lying in the bed of the room Szachon had arranged for him adjacent to Cat's. He reached for the receiver. "Yeah?"

"Szachon here. Is Ms. McCade all right?"

"Yes. Why?"

"I'm worried about Elizabeth."

Jesse sat up and swung his feet to the floor. "Has something else happened?"

"No, but she insists that she's going over to work with Daisy at the plant. I just wanted to tell you that I've hired a permanent bodyguard to stay at the plant with Daisy and Elizabeth."

"You mean, in addition to your security people?"

"Yes. I want someone there as an employee, someone less obvious."

"You want me to recommend somebody?"

"No, I've already got a couple lined up to interview. I just wanted to run this by you. Maybe you could go by the plant and see what you think. Take Cat over. She needs to meet Daisy anyway."

Jesse agreed, then lay back down. Apparently, Szachon was going to include him in the loop. That made his job easier. Finding out who was behind the threats was the way to end his bodyguard assignment.

The way to get away from his growing need for Cat McCade.

7

BY NINE THE NEXT MORNING Cat was still holed away in the bedroom of her suite. Jesse had let himself in with the extra key he had and was waiting in the sitting area. Their clothes had been returned from the cleaners as he'd ordered. He'd pulled on a pair of bikini underwear from the SterlingWear collection, dressed and called his office for an update. There was nothing new to report. Then Cat's suitcases and her cameras were brought down from her old room, followed by a breakfast tray.

Jesse finally knocked on her bedroom door. "Your clothes are here. And breakfast has arrived."

The door opened enough for him to hand the clothes to Cat. "I'll be there in a minute," she said, and took her duffel bag. Moments later, Cat left the bedroom, swallowed a cup of coffee and munched down a sweet roll. She was carrying a small camera as she opened the door and stepped out into the hall. "If you're coming with me, let's go," she called over her shoulder.

That was the extent of their conversation as she headed for the nearest photographic supply shop where she bought a new camera bag and film. From there she worked her way on foot to the construction site where a coffee truck was waiting. She handed the driver what looked like a few bills and he opened for business.

"How'd you manage the breakfast truck?" Jesse asked her, standing away from the food wagon and agonizing over the open target she was making of herself.

"A little charm and a bribe," she answered, and headed toward the building.

The construction site she'd chosen was swarming with men of every description. But it wasn't the coffee truck Cat had hired that attached them like flies to honey, it was Cat. She was wearing a new pair of jeans, running shoes and a simple cotton blouse. They didn't conceal the body beneath.

When Cat McCade said she knew how to satisfy a man, Jesse had thought she was referring to sex. It turned out that, with Cat, doughnuts and a smile were just as potent. She had a way to make a man feel important.

Eventually, Jesse realized that it wasn't an act. Her easy camaraderie with the workers resulted in their standing in line to remove their shirts for her Polaroid camera shots. Once the photos developed, the men were more than willing to write their names and phone numbers on the backs. Good for her, unfortunate for

him. The crowd of workers around Cat was creating a
wall between him and his assignment.

He slid behind the coffee truck and came out closer
to where she was working, biting back a smile when
she shot the overweight and the pimply-faced with as
much enthusiasm as the others. They would never be
in a catalog, but for that moment they were being ogled
by a woman who might never have given them a second glance otherwise.

Then one of the workers noticed Jesse and whispered to another. Soon, the men on the fringes began to
fade away.

"Get over here, Pappy," one of Cat's subjects called.
The man being addressed shook his head. Though still
muscular, his hair and moustache were white and his
skin weathered. "Can't imagine I could sell anything
unless it's Viagra. And I have to tell you, fellas, Pappy
don't need no help there. I got six children and four
grandchildren."

Cat glanced up and grinned at the man. "You probably don't even wear underwear," she joked.

"Sure he does," one of the onlookers joked. "They're
called long johns."

"I don't believe that for a moment," Cat purred.
"Come on, Pappy, let me photograph you." She
walked up and whispered loudly in his ear, "I like

older men, particularly when they have the strong character of a Latin."

While the man was melting under her charm, Jesse cringed. Pappy was a man with a strong character. That certainly didn't apply to him. A man with strength of character would have walked away from making love to Cat a second time. He hadn't. What in hell had happened to his control?

"Is that what you're selling with your pictures, *conchita*?" Pappy asked. "Underwear?"

"Yep, that's what we're selling. And white-haired, older men want their ladies to think they're sexy, too."

Cat shot her photos of Pappy, then stopped to reload while he wrote his name and phone number on the back of his photograph. Afterward, she looked up and found herself alone, except for Jesse.

Cat frowned and looked around. "Where'd everybody go?"

Pappy cocked his head toward Jesse and said, "They don't much like the police. Some of the men, well, they have families in Mexico that depend on their checks. If they're caught, they could be sent back to Mexico."

"He isn't looking for illegals," Cat said, giving Jesse a tilt of her head. "He's working for me."

Pappy smiled. "They don't trust anybody. Me? I'm too old to worry. When I go home and tell my wife I

could be an underwear model, she's gonna burst her
sides laughing.''

"Thank you, Pappy," Cat said, giving him a hug.
"Take this card. I've written my name and number on
the back. Pass the word that nobody has anything to
fear from me. And tell your wife that I may make you
famous."

"I'd rather be rich," Pappy said.

"That, too."

Cat dismissed the coffee truck and headed away
from the building site. "You're going to have to leave
your white shirt, your badge, your gun and your Stetson behind if this is going to work, Ranger, or I'm going to have to go it alone. It's your choice."

"My choice," he snapped, "is for you to stop acting
like you're the chairman of the board and talk to me."

She came to a stop and turned around. "I'm sorry.
What do you want to talk about?"

"To start with, about last night."

"Nope. I've thought about that. From now on I'm
working and you're watching for the bad guys. Anything else is off-limits. No more fun and games."

"Fine with me," he drawled. But why did he have a
strong urge to make her eat those words?

NEAR THE HOTEL, Cat came to an abrupt stop at the
back door of a fast-food restaurant where a delivery

truck was being unloaded. She spent a few minutes convincing a Latino with a big smile who didn't speak English, to pose for her and to sign the back of the Polaroid.

"Hey lady, what about me?" a restaurant employee asked. "I'm a real stud. Don't you want to take my picture?"

"Studs aren't what I'm looking for," she said with a laugh, "but sure." The kitchen help scattered when she pointed her camera in their direction. Apologizing to the owner, she explained once more that Jesse was only her bodyguard. Reluctantly, the workers returned. She finished by photographing a priest who was having coffee with a very pregnant young Mexican woman.

When the restaurant owner insisted they be his guests for lunch, Cat agreed and took a seat in the back booth.

"I'm sorry," Jesse said. "I never intended to interfere with your work. Tomorrow, I promise I'll look like one of those workers. I didn't realize I'd be recognized so easily."

She raised her eyes over the burger she'd just bitten into, chewed lustily, then said, "Jesse, I'm willing to bet that they'd know you're a ranger if you were only wearing your underwear."

"What? Is it stamped on my head?"

"It's stamped on your aura. You're a man in charge.

A man of authority. I doubt you could change it if you tried. It's just you." She tilted her head and smiled wryly. "Which explains why we're bound to clash."

"That description could apply to you, as well." He shook his head. "I don't know how you do it. You're planning to turn an old man and a priest into underwear models? Do they even wear what you're selling?"

"Maybe not yet, but who knows?" Over their burger and fries, she explained. "My proposal suggested to Mr. Szachon that the men who buy sexy lingerie for their women already buy the same kind of thing for themselves. What SterlingWear should tap into is the untouched market, the man who wouldn't normally be a customer, like a Texas Ranger."

"What makes you think Texas Rangers don't already wear this kind of product."

She smiled and quipped, "*You* don't."

And just as suddenly as the morning awkwardness had come, it disappeared.

"You're right," he admitted, and grinned. "If I bother to wear it at all, I just reach into the drawer and pull out whatever's there. When I run out, I go shopping and grab the first thing I see."

"Not if you're wearing SterlingWear," she said.

"Why should my shopping habits change?" he asked defensively.

"Because your women are going to love your sexy

new look and your new wardrobe will be too expensive to discard."

"My women?"

"Well, you're not a monk, are you?"

"No," he said, wondering what she'd think if she knew just how close he was to being celibate. He'd had more sex in the last two days than the past two months. Worse, he'd spent far too much time thinking of making love to Cat McCade than getting to the bottom of the problem that had made him her bodyguard. "But you're going to have to convince me that my underwear makes a difference."

"I'll put you in the catalog and you'll find out."

"No way. I'd never allow my photograph to be in your catalog."

"You wouldn't?"

"I seem to be in enough trouble. I don't want to ask for more."

"Under no circumstances would you pose for me?"

He didn't like the I-don't-believe-you look in her eyes. It matched her self-confidence, if not her words. She dropped any further argument when she looked up at the person entering the lunchroom. It was Pappy. He surveyed the dining area, then made his way over to the priest's table. Giving the young woman already seated a hug, he claimed the empty chair beside her and took her hand.

"Looks like your white-haired model was right. If the girl's his wife, he isn't an old man."

"I don't think she's his wife. A daughter maybe. She's crying."

When Pappy left, the priest gave the girl a farewell pat on the shoulder and followed the potential geriatric underwear model into the street. Cat bounded up and headed after them, leaving Jesse with a half-eaten burger. The last time she'd gotten away from him, she'd ended up in the river.

By the time he caught up, Pappy and the girl were gone and Cat was walking along the river in a deep discussion with the priest.

"Please don't do that again," Jesse snapped, catching her by the arm. "You're in danger, remember?"

"Nonsense," she said, shoving his hand aside. "I'm with a holy man here. Now don't interrupt. Why won't she go home, Father Mulvaney."

"Because she's determined to get a job, stay here and have her baby. Her uncle is very worried. He is already supporting seven family members."

"She looked like she was pretty far along," Cat observed. "Where's the father?"

"The baby's father was killed. Now the grandfather wants the child but not his son's wife. He is a very powerful man in Mexico."

"So," Cat said, "she's here in this country and she's

carrying the child. Possession is nine-tenths of the law, isn't it?"

"It's money," the priest confessed. "She needs to keep a low profile and she's probably not going to be able to hold down a job."

"And you said her uncle can't help her?" Jesse asked.

The priest shook his head. "Rosa's having a hard time. Her uncle, the man you saw at our table, called Pappy, has taken her in, but he already has a houseful of relatives he's supporting. The church will help, of course, but she insists on taking care of herself. That would be admirable but foolish, providing anyone would even hire her."

"Does she know the city?" Cat asked.

"Yes, and she reads and writes English," the priest answered.

"Fine, I'll hire her."

Jesse blanched. "To do what?"

"To be my assistant. To keep you from running off all my candidates. To interpret for me and to catalog my photographs. I always hire a local assistant. Will you speak to her, Father?"

"Or course, if you're sure. She will be very grateful."

"So will I," Cat said. "Ask her if she'll be at the Palace in the morning about nine o'clock. Tell her to ask at the desk for—" she stopped, gave Jesse an odd look and said "—Hazel Smith."

"Not a good idea," Jesse said, shaking his head. "Remember, someone's threatening the women around Szachon. I'm having a hard enough time keeping up with you. I don't need to be responsible for a pregnant woman."

Jesse watched the spark wash out of Cat's face.

"You're right," she agreed. "I wouldn't want to put her in danger, Father. Please ask her to come anyway. I'll find something else for her to do."

On the way back to the hotel Cat was too quiet and uncharacteristically still. "What's on your mind?" Jesse asked her, almost afraid to hear her answer. This was a woman who avoided families and commitment. Now she was offering to take in a pregnant woman she didn't even know. "Being a fairy godmother doesn't seem your style."

"Nothing's on my mind. I mean, I'm just planning tomorrow's schedule. What are you going to do about finding the person sending the threats?"

"Captain Wade told me to leave it up to the city police unless something happens to involve me." She didn't have to know his office was following up, asking questions.

Jesse felt bad about not being honest with Cat, but Captain Wade had given him direct orders not to share the information they were accumulating. So far, all the women in Szachon's past life had been eliminated as suspects. The women had been horrified at the idea that someone was threatening Zon's women. That left someone in the present.

So far nothing had made any sense. Elizabeth wouldn't have anything against Szachon's business—she stood to gain a livelihood. Cat would achieve the professional status she wanted. And Daisy? She was not only an ex-significant other who seemed to genuinely care for Szachon, she was being offered an opportunity that was remarkable. "And what about your involvement in Rosa's problem? I didn't think you were into babies and motherhood."

She ignored his comment. "You're doing nothing to find the culprit? Ranger Dane, why don't I believe that? You're involved in this business, aren't you?"

"You're my business. So, yes, I'm involved."

She eyed him a moment longer, then shrugged. "For now, let's get back to the hotel. I want to take a look at the sample bag of underwear."

"Are you in a hurry, Cat?"

"No. Why?"

"I'd like to check out Daisy's Designs. Our boss said she got a message, too."

"Good idea," Cat agreed. "I'd like to see the design shop, as well. I'll drive the El Camino?"

"*I'll* drive," Jesse said. "I know the area."

"I wonder how I knew you'd say that."

JESSE HEADED for the industrial section of San Antonio on the outskirts of town. He knew vaguely about where the business was located, but it still took a while for him to wind his way to the right place. Instead of a typical factory building, the business was housed in a neat yellow structure complete with shutters and a bay window in the front.

Daisy's Designs was spelled out in green script with white daisies as dots for the *i*s. The parking lot had been freshly paved, with spaces at the door reserved for customers. A woman driving a navy BMW was just leaving.

"Some place," Jesse observed.

"Some place," Cat echoed when they went inside and found themselves in a sea of greenery and fish ponds. There was a receptionist's desk, but no receptionist.

"Hello?" she called. "Anyone here?"

"Come on back," was the feminine response.

A tall brunette, wearing a black body suit and an overblouse was studying fabrics draped over a nude mannequin. "Which do you like?" she asked Cat, flipping a pair of granny grasses from the top of her pixie haircut down to her nose and leaning forward. First she fingered the silver fabric shot with little threads of turquoise and then the aquamarine with tiny inserts of glowing stones.

Cat immediately thought of Audrey Hepburn in *Sabrina*. If this woman was Daisy, she was just as lovely.

"Depends on what you're going to do with it, I guess," Jesse said.

At the sound of his voice the woman turned and then looked at Cat. "I'm sorry. I thought you were Elizabeth. I'm Daisy Easter. What can I do for you?"

Jesse stepped forward and held out his hand. "I'm Ranger Jesse Dane and this is my...associate, Ms. Cat McCade. Is Mrs. Vadin here?"

"No, but she's on her way." Daisy smiled at Cat. "You're the one who is going to shoot Zon's catalog. You have to be good or he wouldn't have chosen you, but I do have to say that you're a Szachon woman."

Cat blinked. "A what?"

"A Szachon woman. I should know, I was one for the most elegant six months of my life. How long have you been the chosen one?"

"I'm his employee, not his woman." Cat's tone was frosty and she assumed by Jesse's expression that he wasn't pleased with Daisy's words. Surely, he wouldn't believe that Szachon was after her, or that she'd be interested if he were.

"Sorry. He has women standing in line. He's kind

and generous and he cares about all his women. This business is my gift for being his girl... Don't look so shocked. He always tells the woman his plan and rewards her when it ends. I knew it going into the relationship and wouldn't have traded it for anything. I liked Zon's honesty and I genuinely like the man."

"And I like my freedom," Cat said. "I'm not interested in anything except working for Mr. Szachon."

Daisy turned to Jesse and smiled. "I can see why."

"Ranger Dane is my bodyguard, nothing else."

"Sure, he is," Daisy agreed. "And what can I do for you, Ranger Dane?"

"You can tell me whether you have an idea who might be trying to sabotage this business."

"Until I heard about Cat's hotel room being trashed I wasn't even sure the trouble was with the business. Now, I don't know. I have no idea. It makes no sense."

"I don't want to alarm you, Daisy," Jesse said, "but you really shouldn't leave the doors open and just invite people in. As impossible as this seems, there could be someone out there determined to do you harm."

"Oh, I'm not worried," she said, "not anymore. I have my own bodyguard." She looked past them to the door.

"Howdy, Jesse."

"Bull? You're her bodyguard?" The bald-headed

man was standing in the door behind Elizabeth. "I thought you worked at the Corral."

"Not anymore. I'm Daisy's new receptionist. And you guys don't have an appointment."

Bull in a cowboy outfit was one thing. But in an embroidered-satin, knee-length shirt, he looked like a refugee from a Charlie Chaplin movie. "Where'd you get that outfit?"

"Daisy made it. Ain't it grand?"

"I'M SURPRISED you didn't ask Bull to pose for you," Jesse said with a grin as they drove back to the hotel.

"I might have if I hadn't been so stunned. He's big, but he isn't fat. Actually, he's just the kind of man who should model the product."

Jesse shook his head. "Maybe, but I'm not certain the world is ready for Bull in a thong."

"Maybe not," Cat agreed.

"I'm still trying to figure out Szachon. He seems to be a nice guy, doesn't pull rank, cares about his family and his employees. The captain says he's doing a lot for the town and he's totally out front and honest. Trust me, that's rare," Jesse said.

"Well, he's honest enough about his women. Be his and he'll reward you." She shook her head. "I could never do that."

"Do what? Belong to someone?"

"No, expect to be paid for my company. Anybody who wants me has to be someone I want in return. If I wanted *anyone*, that is."

"But you don't want anybody, do you, Cat? Why is that?"

"I never met anybody I could trust to understand and respect me for who I am." She gave him a sidelong glance. "What about you?"

He came to a traffic light and stopped. After a long moment he answered. "I hope you know that you can trust me. I never lie and I would never try to change the woman I love."

"Have you ever been in love, Jesse?"

The light changed and Jesse gave the gas pedal a push, grateful for the movement. "No, I've never been in love."

No explanations, no excuses. Only the promise that he didn't lie and would never change his woman. Cat shivered. That was too much to believe. Jesse James Dane was too much to believe. His mother had named him right. He was a thief. And she was in danger of having her heart stolen.

"What about you, Cat? You ever been in love?"

"No. Never let myself. One-night stands—maybe a day or two—that's my limit." *Except with you.* She didn't like what was happening here. She was tied to a man who was a danger to the life she'd created for herself.

"In other words, you never give yourself a chance," Jesse said, knowing what her answer would be. "What do you suppose would happen if you quit running?"

"I don't intend to find out," she said softly. "Why don't we get something to eat before we go back to the hotel?"

"Sure, what do you want?"

"I don't know, barbecue?" But she did know. She wanted Jesse and the longer they stayed away from the hotel, the better.

"Barbecue, it is," Jesse said, and drove to a place that looked like a shack. Tables were set outside under trees that were lit by lanterns. The owner, Manuel, knew Jesse and welcomed him and his *"señorita."*

"It has been too long, Ranger Dane," Manuel said. "My Estelle thinks you have forgotten us."

Jesse put his hand on Cat's back as naturally as if they were two people out for an evening. "You know I'd never forget Estelle. Tell her we've come for some of her ribs."

They'd barely taken their seats when a plump woman wearing a red dress and an apron came bustling out of the back. "Jesse! Jesse! Where have you been?"

She hugged the ranger, then stood back and examined Cat. "Aha! Now I see. You've finally found a *señorita*." She caught Cat's hand and held it for a moment, gazed at her sternly, then stood back. "You've chosen well, my friend. She is worth the wait. When is the wedding to be?"

"But..."Cat began, "I'm not. I mean, there is no wedding."

Estelle patted her cheek and gave Jesse a kiss. "But there will be. I know about these things. The first time I met Ranger Dane he told me he'd find my boy and bring him home. He did. He's a man of honor, a strong man, who needs a strong woman." She gave Jesse a nod and left.

"Does every woman in Texas think you walk on water?"

"Nope. You don't."

Cat rolled her eyes at that, then asked, "Where was her son?"

"He just got in with the wrong crowd and couldn't figure out how to get out. I found him down in Houston and brought him home. He was so glad to be back that he turned over a new leaf. Had nothing to do with me."

They ate spicy barbecue and slaw, and drank margaritas. Soon the wandering musicians tuned up and walked among the crowd playing sorrowful love songs for the couples and lively Spanish music for the others.

Everything about the evening was romantic. Too romantic, Cat decided, and pushed back from the table. "I think we'd better go."

"Not until you have one dance," Estelle said, appearing at Cat's side. "No man worth his salt takes a *señorita* out without dancing under the stars."

Jesse smiled and took Cat's hand. "Let's go, Cinderella. Let's make her happy."

Whether it was the stars, the drinks, or something else, Cat gave in to the music and melted against Jesse. The feeling of being cherished was new. For a long moment she wished it was real. One song turned into two and, finally, when she looked up, they were the only ones still there.

"I think we'd definitely better go," she said. "Otherwise, I'm going to fall asleep right here and you're going to have to carry me to bed."

"My pleasure," Jesse said, and wished he didn't mean it.

8

To Jesse's surprise, the ambience of the evening held fast as they returned to the hotel. He opened the door to the suite and entered, keeping Cat behind him. Once he'd determined that they were alone, he turned around. Cat leaned against him for a moment, kissed him, then pulled back and whispered, "Good night, Jesse James Dane. You do know how to show a girl a good time."

"It doesn't have to be over yet," he said.

"I think it does. Thank you for the romantic evening, but the clock has chimed midnight. My coach has turned back into a pumpkin and the fantasy has to end."

"But what happens to the prince? I don't even have a glass slipper."

"The prince turns back into a Texas Ranger and his kingdom returns to being the State of Texas. And it can't be any other way." She pushed herself away, turned and went into her room. "We both know this isn't real," she said, and closed the door.

This isn't real. Good advice, Dane. The woman might

be a fantasy but every cell in his body throbbed with real feeling, not just desire but longing. He was beginning to understand that this was something more powerful than he could simply dismiss.

Cat had to feel the same thing. She'd convinced herself that she could do just fine alone. But somehow, underneath her wise-ass confidence, he sensed she was a woman who needed to be loved. He didn't know where they were headed but, for now, he'd wait for her to figure it out.

Waiting wasn't that easy, though. The night was endless. Total silence came from the other side of the adjoining wall. Apparently he was the only one unable to sleep.

The situation, whatever it was, needed to be settled; he needed to get back to a normal life. But instead of going after the bad guy, he was stuck here with the source of his acute discomfort. He tried to ignore the army of ants that seemed to be marching up his backbone. He knew the captain was running a check, but he wondered if Szachon had contacted Elizabeth's husband. Granted, he was in Europe and there was no indication that he was concerned or opposed to Elizabeth's being here. But what did Szachon know? And how was he going to find out? After hours of pacing the sitting area of his room, Jesse verified that Szachon had planted a security officer in the hall as he'd directed and moved to the bedroom where he finally drifted into a short, restless sleep.

By 8:00 a.m. he was showered and dressed. While he refused to go anywhere without his pistol, he'd otherwise followed Cat's directions. He'd shed his badge and Stetson. The new white shirt he'd bought downstairs was fresh and clean, but his pants were wrinkled and his boots were scuffed. He hadn't thought to pick up razors, so he had no choice but to keep the stubble of a beard. He certainly didn't look like a Texas Ranger; his outlaw name, Jesse James, was closer to the truth.

Cat was no late sleeper, either. He could hear her moving around and talking on the phone in her room. By eight-thirty, he knocked on her door and walked in as she was ordering room service. All business this morning, she asked, "Anything new, Ranger?"

"Nothing." He picked up some brochures and ruffled them, slapping them against his knee.

"You'd rather be looking for the bad guy, wouldn't you?"

He thought about his answer. "I'd like to be in on the investigation, yes. Being a bodyguard isn't my duty of choice. How long do you think this job will take?"

"Why, are you tired of protecting me?"

"Tired? Yes. How did you sleep last night?"

"I slept well," she lied. "You?"

"Not much, but that's the way of it when you're responsible for someone's safety. You have to keep one eye open."

"Jesse, maybe you'd better stay here today, get some rest. I'll have Szachon send one of his men with Rosa and me so you won't have to worry."

Jesse shook his head. "You're going to be safe with a woman almost eight months' pregnant? Where do you plan to go, the hospital?"

"Well, hospitals could be a choice hunting ground." She tossed another packet of brochures onto the couch nearest Jesse. "But these—" she handed him her folders "—are some of the places I want to check out. I thought we'd start with the Alamo."

He flipped through all eleven of the brochures, then dropped them onto the table. "And I thought you were looking for ordinary men to be your models. Why are we going to the Alamo? It's full of tourists."

"At this point, I'm looking for good background, as well."

Jesse gave a disbelieving laugh. "I give up. You're the photographer, but somehow I don't see Davy Crockett and Jim Bowie defending the Alamo in their underwear."

"Mr. Szachon's contract allows me to choose the settings for the catalog as well as the models. I intend to shoot the men in their ordinary lives. The idea is to suggest that every man is a SterlingWear candidate. I also want to check out that park that tells the story of Texas on a limestone quarry wall."

"Fiesta Texas," he said, shaking his head. "Great! A two-hundred-acre theme park full of tourists. Protecting you will be a piece of cake there."

The phone rang at the same time there was a knock on the door.

Jesse glanced at his watch. It was five minutes to nine. He checked the peephole and let in the bellman, who carried an enormous breakfast tray, then picked up the phone.

"This is Owen at the front desk. There is a woman here named Rosa who says Hazel Smith is expecting her."

Jesse laughed. "She is. Please have her escorted up to the room." He turned to Cat. "Your assistant is here," he said, and watched her jut her chin forward as if to dare him to disagree.

"As a member of law enforcement, I have to say you really ought to think about this business with Rosa," Jesse said, pouring a cup of coffee. "It's probably going to be more a matter of you assisting her than the other way around."

"Don't be silly," she said, secretly wondering if he was right. Offering Rosa a job had seemed to be a good thing at the time.

"You could be putting her in danger. Have you thought about that?"

"Look, Jesse, I don't know what's going on here, but I don't think I'm in danger. Besides, there'll be three of us."

"Three would be good," he answered. "But considering how far along she is, it's four I'm worried about. It was a nice gesture, giving her a job as your assistant, but it really is a risk, particularly when we're out in the open."

"You may be right," she finally agreed. "Today, I'll leave her here, cataloging the photographs. I can do without her. We'll go to Szachon's ranch first. I'm looking for background there and real cowboys."

Jesse let Rosa in. He finally realized why Cat had ordered so much food to be delivered and had delayed the eating of it. It was for Rosa. When Rosa wouldn't eat unless Cat and Jesse did, Cat polished off coffee and a bagel while Jesse downed a couple of sweet rolls and juice.

Cat gathered up her equipment, encouraging the expectant mother to finish the rest of the food while she and Jesse were gone. "When you're finished eating, Rosa, the Polaroid photographs on the desk should be placed in protective plastic-jacketed sheets. I'd like you to answer the phone until about three o'clock in case any of my potential models call. Just take the name and number. After that, you're free to go. Tomorrow we'll go to the Alamo."

"You don't need me to accompany you today?" Rosa asked, puzzled. "I promise I will be no problem, *señorita,*" she assured her. "Please?" she pleaded almost tearfully. "I will take care of your clothes, your—" she looked around helplessly "—your things. Whatever you want."

"That won't be necessary," Cat explained.

Questions filled Rosa's eyes. "Then what do you need from Rosa?"

"I really want you to help me make the men I'll be shooting feel comfortable."

"Men?" Rosa cut a quick glance at Jesse. "Señor Dane is one of these men?"

"Oh, he's not my man!" Cat said quickly. An unwelcome heat flushed her face at her words. "I mean—"

"Oh. I think that is too bad," Rosa said.

JESSE CALLED SZACHON and asked him to approve their trip to his ranch, then contacted the garage so that his truck was outside when they reached the lobby. Cat didn't have to know that he now had a weapon in the glove compartment.

They left San Antonio behind for the open grasslands. The ranch was half an hour out of San Antonio. Jesse felt more comfortable already. Photographing real working cowboys on Szachon's spread would be a safer situation than the nightclub they'd gone to. But it was more than that. Cat didn't say anything and neither did he, and this time the silence was comfortable. Jesse started to relax.

That's when he noticed the white truck following them. One front fender had been primed for painting. He couldn't read the license plate but every time he slowed down, so did the truck.

It kept a respectful distance back, matching the pace of the Ram. Jesse didn't mention their shadow to Cat. If the person driving had wanted to do them harm, he'd have plenty of opportunity.

Szachon's spread made the Ewing's Southfork on Dallas look like a factory-built home. A white fence lined the road for miles, ending in white brick columns joined by a wrought-iron arch. A voice on the intercom connected to the house announced their permission to enter and the iron gate opened. In his rearview mirror, Jesse watched as the truck passed the entrance to the house, throwing up a cloud of dust in its wake. Once it was out of sight, Jesse drove up to the house and around the back to the stables.

"This is some spread," Cat said.

Jesse brought the truck to a stop under a tree next to the corral. Beyond the fences, flat, brown earth spread out as far as he could see. In the far distance cattle bunched together grazing lazily in the sunlight. "I wonder how often Zon spends the night here. He doesn't seem to be a cattle man."

A weathered, silver-haired man wearing riding pants came out of the barn and headed toward them. He was smiling. "Hello. I'm Solton Szachon, Zon's father. You must be Catherine." He held out his hand. "Call me Solly."

Cat nodded. "You're his father?" she asked in amazement.

"Yep. I thought you might be Zon's new lady, but I can see you're spoken for." He turned to Jesse. "You'd be that young ranger, the one who found the undertaker's wife." He shook Jesse's hand.

"Yes, sir. Solton Szachon. I can't quite place the name or the accent."

"Poland, son. My father came to Texas on a freighter, married Zon's grandmother and stayed. My mother was Texas oil money and folks never did understand what she saw in my father. She loved him but she couldn't live with him. When she died, her oil money became Szachon money. We Szachons seem to be able to hang on to our money longer than our women."

Cat looked around. "And Mrs. Szachon?"

Solly laughed. "Ah, my dear. I married a hothouse flower. After five years of being unfulfilled, she had

Zon. The next year, she took off to Europe and found culture and a new husband."

"I'm sorry, Solly," Cat said, "I didn't mean to pry."

"No problem. Everybody knows. Makes it easier to work together if you just throw it all out there," Solly admitted.

"And Elizabeth is her child," Jesse said. "And Zon's half sister."

"Yep. Doesn't know it yet, but she's a chip off the old block. She's into culture just like her mother," Solly said, a suggestion of bitterness in his voice. "Zon feels responsible for her and every other woman he comes in contact with. But Elizabeth—" he nodded thoughtfully "—she'll surprise herself one of these days."

As they walked through the barn, Solly pulled pieces of carrots from his vest pocket and stopped to reward each horse with a carrot sliver and a pat on the head.

"You never married again?" Cat asked.

"Nope. The Szachons marry once. Elizabeth's got to go back home and lay down the law to her husband. 'Course, that'd put an end to SterlingWear. What about you two?"

"Both Cat and I have bypassed the white picket fence in the suburbs, as well."

The old man grinned, looking from one to the other. "So far. Too bad, you'd make fine-looking children."

Cat opened her camera bag and pulled out her camera. "I assume your son explained what I'd like to do."

"Zon told me you were coming to take pictures of the hands. I don't know how many we can find, but—say, do you ride?"

"Does a ranger ride?" Jesse grinned. "It's required."

"What about you, Catherine?" Solly asked.

"Well, I've been on a horse a couple of times, but I'm no rider. And call me Cat."

"Good enough. I have a horse that a baby could ride."

"I'm not sure..." Cat began.

"It will be easier if we go to the men, but if you'd rather, we can wait for them to come in from the range. They're moving a herd from one pasture to another."

"A trail drive?" Cat said in awe. "I'd love to see it, but I really am just here to photograph your cowboys."

Solly laughed. "I don't think you'd call this a cattle drive. It's more an afternoon stroll. Buck!" he shouted, pulling on his riding gloves. "Saddle my horse and one for the ranger and old Smokey for Ms. McCade."

Before Cat knew how it happened, the three of them were leaving the barn and heading through the gate that led to the pasture.

"You sure about this?" Jesse asked Cat in a low voice. "I think we can drive the truck anywhere we need to go."

"I think we'd best keep our host happy. I may not be able to walk tomorrow, but I'm willing to give this a try. Solly," she called, nudging her horse forward, "would you allow me to photograph you?"

"Me? Whatever for? I thought you were working on the catalog for my granddaughter's underwear business. I've seen some of that underwear. Do you know what would happen if I wore one of those little scraps of material and sat on a horse all day?"

Jesse thought of the thongs he'd seen in the sample bag and grinned. "The same thing that would happen to me if I rode a motorcycle all day while wearing them."

"Come on, guys," Cat protested. "Don't you want to help make Elizabeth's business a success?"

"I think you're asking the wrong person, little lady. Don't matter what I think. The one giving you the answer to that question ought to be Elizabeth. Why are you taking my picture?"

"A photographer never lets a good shot get away. Who knows, Solly? We might put you in the sales brochure. I already have one model about your age."

"A model my age?"

"Well, he isn't a model, he's a construction worker."

"Young lady, I don't know anything about catalogs or photographs, but I'm not too old to say what I think."

"And what would that be?"

He directed his horse down a little rise and through a stand of trees through which a little stream meandered before he answered. "You're pointing that camera at the wrong target. If you want a man to sell Elizabeth's underwear, you need to look closer to home. But from the way you two look at each other, you already know that, don't you?"

Cat's heart started a rapid, rumbling thump. Was it so obvious that they'd made love? No, not made love, had sex. That's all it had been—sex. The best sex she'd ever had. She'd spent several hours last night trying to recall at least one man who compared with Jesse. There wasn't one. She stuck the photograph of Solly into her pocket. He had a point. So far, she couldn't even remember the faces of the men she'd slept with. None of them lived up to Jesse.

On the other side of the creek, they rode through more trees, then headed into the pasture where eight meandering steers were being herded by two riders who didn't seem to be in any bigger of a hurry than the cattle. The steers stopped at the creek to drink and the cowboys climbed down to let their horses quench their thirst.

"Afternoon, boys," Solly said. "How'd you like to be famous?"

"Did one of us win the lottery?" one of them asked.

He pulled off his hat and bumped it against his knee, sending dust flying. The bandanna tied around his neck made a cooling towel as he dipped it into the creek and wiped the grime from his face and neck.

As he peeled his shirt back, Cat realized she had a problem. Unlike the construction workers who worked under a roof, a long summer of being outdoors had turned the cowboys the color of raisins, except where their shirts covered them. There was no way these cowboys could model underwear unless they used body makeup. But it was possible they might be willing.

"Which one of us won the jackpot?" the other man asked.

"Sorry, boys," Cat said, giving them a genuine smile. The men might not be right, but she might as well shoot some possible location spots. "No jackpot. You remember that commercial a few years ago where the construction worker took a break and drank a soft drink? Well, I'm a photographer looking for men like him, real men who are willing to become underwear models."

"Let me get this straight," the first man said. "You want us to model men's underwear?"

"I don't think my wife would agree," the other said. "But, hey, if it pays good enough, I'll consider it."

"Well, I can't promise you a job. I'm simply collecting possible candidates for a catalog. A committee will make the final choice. What do you say, guys? Want to model underwear?"

"Only if you're wearing yours," the older one answered, climbing back onto his horse. "What do you say, lady?"

"Just a minute," Jesse snapped. "This is a lady, not some bartender in a two-bit roadhouse."

"Hold on, fella," Solly said. "Boys, don't be disrespectful. I told Ms. McCade you wouldn't want the money if you had to pose in your underwear, but she insisted that you have the opportunity."

"We don't get paid for posing unless we get picked?" Buck asked.

"That's right," Cat answered. "I can't promise anything except that I do this all the time. I'll make it as comfortable for you as possible."

By the time she'd finished snapping the photographs, the two men were over their initial embarrassment and suggesting places on the ranch where they could be photographed.

Cat glanced over at Jesse and caught the amusement in his expression. She also noticed how he'd stepped back and let her do her job without interfering. His cooperation was appreciated. She'd found few men who were comfortable with her dealing with male models.

Later, as they rode back to the barn, Cat surreptitiously photographed Jesse. As the snapshot developed itself, she felt a rush of her pulse. The cowboy was right. No question about it, Jesse would be a perfect choice for the catalog.

"Thank you, Solly," Cat said as they rode into the barnyard. "I hope we didn't take up too much of your time."

"Not at all. Come back when you aren't working and we'll roast a pig." He slid down from his horse.

Jesse appeared at Cat's side. "I'll help you," he said, placing his hands around her waist. Solly took the reins and held the horse steady as Jesse lifted her down. Expecting her feet to operate properly, she started to step back and stumbled. Jesse caught her, lifting her against him to steady her.

Her fingertips rested against the cords in his neck and she felt the beat of his pulse. For a moment they stood as if they'd been melded together.

"Just stand still for a few minutes, Cat," Solly said, handing off the horse to one of the hands. "To the inexperienced, riding a horse is like being a sailor on a ship. If you don't have your sea legs, when you step onto dry land, you can be unsteady."

She shook her head. What on earth was she doing, going into a swoon over Jesse with everyone watching? "Sorry, I think it was the swaying. Made me a little dizzy. Thank you, Ranger," she said, pushing herself away. "And thank you, too, Solly. We'd love to come back for a visit."

She headed for the truck, opened the door and stopped dead-still. "Jesse."

Jesse had rounded the driver's side and opened his door. Her voice caught his attention. "What's wrong?"

"Don't you see it?"

"See what?"

"That's my camera case, the one that was stolen when someone broke into my room."

He followed her gaze. The bag had been hung over the mirror. He turned around and surveyed the area. The hands had gone back to their chores and Solly was heading for the house.

"Get in," Jesse said. He'd send someone back to ask questions. For now, he wanted to get Cat away from here. Lifting the bag down with a stick, he pushed it under his seat. "We'll have it checked out when we get back to town."

"I don't understand this," Cat said, beginning to feel worried. "Why would anyone want to frighten me?"

"I haven't figured that out yet."

"Well, I know this—I'm not going to let them, or him or her, get to me. This job is important to me. I think it's time we got involved. What do you think, Jesse? You're a ranger. What would you do if this was your case? Can you catch the bad guy?"

"I don't know yet, but I'm going to find out. Lock the door and stay here. I'm going to talk to Solly."

"Oh, no. You aren't leaving me here." She followed Jesse to the house, only to see Solly stop and turn back.

"Something wrong?" he asked.

"I'm not sure," Jesse asked. "Can you find out if anybody has been seen around my truck?"

"The only one here was Buck, and he seems to be missing."

About that time Buck came riding down the drive at a fast pace. "Solly," he said as he reined his horse to a stop, "there was a white truck stopped up on the road. I rode up to check him out and he took off."

Jesse frowned. "Did the truck have one gray-primed fender?"

"Yeah. You know who it was?" Buck asked.

"No. Did you see which way the truck went?" Jesse asked.

"Back toward the freeway. It's gone now. I let him get away, but folks always stop up on the road and take pictures. I didn't think too much about it until I saw somebody come out of the trees and jump in the truck. Then it roared off down the road."

"Man or woman?" Jesse asked.

"Man, I'd say. But it could have been a woman wearing a baseball cap."

"Solly," Jesse ordered, "take Cat inside. I'm going to

call Zon." He turned to Cat. "You may need to give up your photographing until we find out who the bad guys are."

"No," Cat protested. "If somebody's trying to scare me, they're going to find out that I won't be intimidated. Let's go check out the Alamo."

Jesse put his hands on Cat's shoulders. "No! We need to slow down and think about this."

"I don't need to think. I have a job to do."

"And so do I."

"Sure. I'm your job, remember?"

Cat pulled out of his arms and strode behind Solly toward the back of the house. He was right. She was just a job for him. The feeling of being part of a team, of being close to him, instantly vanished. She wasn't certain whether she was angry at how quickly his entire manner had changed or at herself for allowing him to think he could make decisions for her.

She could have told him that she'd been in danger at other times in her life and survived. She could have told him that she didn't want to be a job. But she'd felt an unwanted fear when she'd seen that bag. Because at that moment she'd realized that Jesse could be in as much danger as she was. If anything happened to him, it would be her fault.

She couldn't begin to explain her concern to Jesse. She wanted to say, "Stay with me until this is over," and that was almost as frightening as the threat. The best thing for her to do was to get away.

She could feel Jesse watching her go inside. Her anger had to be obvious in her stride. He knew he was taking charge, overriding her wishes, giving orders. But he had to be shaking inside to think that someone could get this close—someone who could have done real damage if he'd wanted to. Ranger Jesse James Dane had been hired to protect Cat. Suppose he failed.

9

CAT FOLLOWED Solly into the house, breathing deeply, teeth clenched. A pain in her chest filled her with trembling weakness. Jesse'd lulled her into thinking they were partners, but they weren't. It was all an act; pretending that they were equals, each respecting the other's authority and expertise.

Without discussion, he'd instantly taken charge. He was a man, a Texas Ranger, and he gave orders and expected her to follow them. And she had.

She had.

Now that she was inside the house, she felt the full force of her failure. Jesse felt responsible for her safety, but he was wrong. She'd looked after herself since she was a teen. And she could certainly look after herself now.

"Would you like some iced tea?" Solly asked.

"No. I mean, yes, I think I would."

Moments later they were sipping the cooling beverage inside a plant-filled sunroom.

"You know that someone's threatening your son's women," Cat said.

"My son's women?" Solly laughed. "For the first time in a while, Zon doesn't have even one woman. Since Elizabeth came, he's spent all his time with her."

Cat started to explain the scope of the term "women" and thought better of it. She stood and walked over to the wall of glass that looked out over a pool and a set of weathered swings. "Elizabeth isn't your daughter, but I get the feeling that you're close."

"We are. She should have been mine, but she isn't. From the time she was just a little thing, she's visited the ranch every summer. At least until she married. The pool and the swings were built for her. We spent many hours together out there, but since she came back here this time, she's changed. She seems lost."

"What happened between Elizabeth and her husband?" Cat asked.

"I don't ask questions. But I think some European men believe that a measure of their success is having a wife, children *and* a mistress. Maybe if Elizabeth had had a child..."

There were too many maybes. Normally, Cat went into her projects with a plan that she carried out with reasonable efficiency before moving on to the next one. It didn't seem to be happening this time. She'd allowed herself to be drawn into a complicated set of relationships that had clouded her vision.

She could still see that camera bag hanging there. It

was more than a warning; it was as if she was being taunted. Everything was different. Maybe she ought to forget about SterlingWear and take the previous assignment she'd been offered, to photograph Native Americans for a fund-raising calendar.

No, damn it. She'd never been a quitter and she wouldn't be now. She wouldn't allow Jesse to leave her with Solly. He'd brought her to the ranch in his truck. She should have known better than to let him do that. If she were traveling in the El Camino, she could leave on her own. Well, she'd learned her lesson.

Thanking Solly, she headed back to the truck where Jesse was punching numbers into his cell phone.

JESSE HOPED he was doing the right thing when he dialed the hotel. "Mr. Szachon, we've had a little situation out here."

"What happened, Dane?"

"Someone left the camera bag stolen from Cat's room hanging over the mirror in my truck. Someone got that close and I didn't even know it. I don't like this. It could have been a bomb. I thought you might want to alert your security force."

"Oh, my God. Is Cat all right?"

"She seems to be," Jesse answered. "She's a tough woman. I think whoever did this may have followed us from town."

"That settles it. Bring her back to the hotel. The catalog is going on hold until we figure this out."

"I don't think she's going to like that," Jesse said as he ended the conversation and pressed the end button on his cell phone.

"Like what?" Cat asked as she opened the passenger side door and climbed into Jesse's truck.

"Our employer says that we have to come back to the hotel. He's putting a hold on SterlingWear until we get to the bottom of this."

"He can't do that."

"You tell him. I'm just following orders."

Cat slammed the door. "You're bent on following orders, aren't you?"

"I try to. I find that in the long run, that's generally better."

"You mean that you use them to justify your decisions." Cat was mad enough to spit. Mad that Jesse played his rules card when he needed it, then did what he decided was necessary. Well, she could do that, as well. They'd go back to the hotel. Jesse would be relieved of his duty and she'd get on with her work. With him out of her life, she'd have control again. There were other jobs, but this one would make her career. It combined the kind of photography she was best at with an ongoing, year-round product. Her mind was set on fast-forwarding her career in a way it hadn't been before.

Now some idiot was trying to stop the project.

That had to be the key. "Jesse, maybe we should be concentrating on the angle that all this is happening to keep SterlingWear from becoming a success."

"I've been thinking about that myself."

Fired with her own observations, Cat went on. "I mean, nobody has been hurt and they could have been. Every move has been more in the nature of a warning than a real threat. They didn't do any damage to my cameras or to the factory. And you said yourself, the culprit seems to be toying with us."

"I noticed that the focus seems to have changed to you," Jesse said.

"But why me instead of Elizabeth? He could get to Elizabeth, too, if he wanted to. Why hasn't he done it?"

"Because your contribution may be the key to success and you are making yourself an open target. He thinks he can get to you."

THE DESK CLERK intercepted them when they entered the lobby. Mr. Szachon wanted them to come directly to his office.

The man waiting there with Zon was a stranger. "Ranger Dane," Szachon greeted, standing behind his desk. "This is Raoul Vadin, Elizabeth's husband. I notified him about what's been happening and he flew over on the Concorde."

Jesse held out his hand. "Good to meet you, sir. I'm sorry about the threats to your wife."

"So am I." Vadin's tone was brisk, but there was worry in his voice. "I never expected her to leave London and come here. Now she's in danger. I'm going to take her home."

"And," Zon went on, "this is Catherine McCade, Elizabeth's photographer and catalog designer."

Dark, mysterious, definitely French, Cat could see how he could mesmerize with his eyes. A woman could fall under his spell. She could see why Elizabeth married him so quickly.

"Ms. McCade has been threatened, too," Zon continued.

Vadin shifted his eyes to her. "You were hurt?"

"No. Someone just likes to play games. We suspect it's an attempt to prevent SterlingWear from becoming a reality."

"I'm in favor of that," Vadin said.

"Where's Elizabeth?" Jesse asked.

Zon shook his head. "I sent for her. She ought to be here soon."

"You kidnapped her once, I hope you haven't done it again," Vadin snapped.

"She's the one who called me, Vadin," Szachon

stressed. "She wanted to come home and needed a job and a place to live. I came up with SterlingWear. As president, Elizabeth would have her own business and an entire new life. She seemed excited about that."

"I'll admit, Elizabeth has been out of sorts. We'd been having problems, but we were working through them," Vadin conceded. "Elizabeth wouldn't be here, Zon, if it weren't for your help."

Zon scoffed. "What do you mean? Elizabeth is my sister. Why shouldn't I help her?" He turned away from Raoul. "Since all three of the women involved in the project have been threatened, I agree. It has something to do with SterlingWear."

"We need to assume that," Jesse said. "Frankly, Mr. Szachon, if we're going to find out, it's time you bring me into the loop officially. I don't mean for you to release me from protecting Cat, but allow me to work with the local police officers so that I can check out some ideas."

"That's not necessary," Cat said. "Why not just publicly announce that the project has been canceled. If that's what the slimeball is going for, he'll think his plan has worked. Elizabeth, Daisy and I can go about our business without bodyguards while you look for the person behind the threats."

"There's another way," Zon said. "All the threats

have been to the women around me. If I send Elizabeth and Catherine away, that will solve the problem."

Cat caught her breath. "You can't do that. This catalog is my project. We have a contract. I'll hold you to it."

"What about this?" Jesse suggested. "You announce publicly that the women will be replaced with men. Then we'll be able to tell whether the trouble is with the women or the project."

"So, Jesse, do you intend to take a quick course in photography?" Cat asked, making no attempt at concealing her fury at the man who'd been pushing all her buttons from the moment she'd first laid eyes on him.

"Of course not," he protested. "But surely there must be male photographers who do what you do."

"There are. But not as well."

Zon left his position behind the desk and walked toward Cat. "He has a good idea. You wouldn't be expected to lose the income from the contract," he said. "I would, of course, pay you what we agreed upon."

"No," she said quietly. "I earn my money. Thank you, anyway, Mr. Szachon. This was almost perfect." She turned around to leave the room, glaring at Jesse who reached out to stop her. "Don't, Ranger Dane. Oh, and by the way, you still haven't sent me the bill for your bike. If you'll prepare it, I'll take care of the charges before I leave."

She brushed past him and out into the foyer, glancing at Raoul Vadin as she left. Elizabeth had had plenty of time to get to the hotel, yet she hadn't. Was she rebelling in her own way, or was she avoiding her husband?

Cat stepped into the elevator. She needed to figure out what she would do about Rosa. The woman would never get a real job this far into her pregnancy. Cat couldn't pay Rosa's salary if *she* didn't get paid. But there was more than one way to sell her work. The Native American fund-raising calendar would tide her over. That would get her out of San Antonia, away from Jesse. Rosa could go with her.

"Cat," Jesse called, "wait. It isn't safe for you to go off alone."

But the elevator door closed and she escaped, at least temporarily.

"LET HER GO, Dane," Szachon said. "One of my men is still down on her floor. I'd like to talk to you about the situation."

Reluctantly, Jesse stepped back. He didn't think Cat was in mortal danger, but she was a headstrong woman who knew no fear.

"Yes, sir."

For the next hour they batted ideas back and forth. Vadin didn't seem to have much to contribute. He was convinced that Zon had hidden Elizabeth away. "Where is she, Szachon? My wife doesn't have the gumption to take off on her own."

Jesse didn't argue but he wanted to say, "She left you and came here." But he didn't. And he was growing more and more antsy about where she was and about Cat being left alone. Finally he stood. "I'm sorry, Mr. Szachon, but I really think I ought to check on Cat. My opinion is that it would be wise to make it public that the SterlingWear project is being put on hold for now—give us some breathing room."

"Of course, Ranger. I don't know what will happen, but if you don't mind I'd like you to stay on until we get to the bottom of this. I'll speak to your superior."

Jesse nodded and headed down to the fifteenth floor. There was no guard on the floor. In fact everything was quiet—too quiet. He knocked on the door of Cat's suite, waited, then inserted the key.

He knew the minute he opened the door that there was no one here. Cat's camera bag and cameras were gone, along with her duffel bag. The brochures were still on the table beside the couch. He glanced at them, trying to decide if any were missing. But he couldn't be certain. A long minute passed before he realized that Rosa was gone, too.

Rosa!

He headed for the elevator, his heart in his throat.

Where had Cat gone? When the elevator doors opened, the security guard stepped out.

"Where is she?" Jesse demanded.

"Who?"

"Ms. McCade."

"I don't know. She said Mr. Szachon wanted me upstairs. I made certain they had the door locked and went up. He said it was a mistake and I should get back down here."

"How long ago?"

"Five, maybe ten, minutes ago."

Jesse stepped inside the elevator and hit the lobby button. "Get in," he told the guard. "You go down to the parking deck and see if her El Camino is there. If not, find out if the attendant knows anything."

"Where're you going?" the guard asked.

"To the lobby to ask questions."

When they reached the lobby, Jesse dashed across to the concierge's desk. "Have you seen Ms. McCade?"

"No, sir. Would you like me to page her?"

Shaking his head, Jesse moved on to the front desk, asking the same question and getting the same answer. "She'd be with a Mexican woman—a pregnant Mexican woman."

"No, sir."

"What about Mrs. Vadin?"

The answer was the same.

Jesse had never felt so helpless. Where would she have gone? His gaze moved past the rack of tourist brochures. In minutes he'd matched the brochures still on the table in the suite. And then he saw it—the Alabama-Coushatta Indian reservation, the folder had been missing from Cat's stack. He didn't know why, but for whatever reason, that's where she was headed.

He made his way to the parking garage and soon pulled his truck out onto the road. The reservation was northeast of San Antonio. She didn't know the area so she'd take the route on the brochure. By using a couple of shortcuts, he ought to be able to catch her—if he'd guessed right. He'd reach the main highway about the time she'd get there.

He put his foot on the gas, his heart in his throat. What if he'd guessed wrong? He was breaking still another rule by not notifying the captain. Cat McCade was going to be his downfall.

No, he admitted. She wasn't *going* to be his downfall. She already *was*. He couldn't even think straight when she was around. It was even worse when she wasn't. Now she'd put herself in danger. He didn't allow himself to think about losing her. He'd think about keeping her later.

The side road he was taking merged into the main highway. And just ahead was the El Camino. He let out a deep sigh of relief.

Jesse's truck was outfitted with every piece of information, equipment or tool a ranger would need, except the holster he'd left back in the hotel. At least he had his ankle weapon and a pistol in the glove box. He debated about notifying the captain, then reached over and took the pistol out. He'd just let her go. This was as good a way as any to keep her away from Szachon's trouble.

That's when he saw it—the white truck with the gray-primed front fender.

10

"WHERE IS RANGER DANE?" Rosa asked as they motored down the road toward the reservation.

"He will not be accompanying me any longer, Rosa."

"You are angry with him?"

"No. What makes you think I'm angry?"

Rosa smiled. "Only two things would make you hold the steering wheel like that. Anger or fear. And I don't think you are afraid of anything."

Cat looked down at her hands. They were gripping the wheel so tightly that her knuckles were white. Rosa was wrong. She was afraid, very afraid. She had become much too involved with Jesse. Even when she wasn't with him, he was constantly on her mind.

"It's the traffic," Cat finally said. She took a deep breath and forced herself to relax.

The traffic heading toward the reservation was already heavy. Cat glanced at Rosa and hoped she was doing the right thing. "I really admire you, Rosa. I could never have a baby alone."

"I do what I have to do."

"I understand the grandfather wants your baby."

"Only if the child is a boy."

Cat felt as if she'd stepped back to her childhood. If she'd been a boy, her father would have cared about her. He'd have turned her into a re-creation of himself. But she'd taken her chances on the world and she'd escaped. She had always known that as long as she didn't get too close to anyone, she'd be fine.

But she *had* gotten too close and she wasn't at all fine.

"Does he know where you are?" Cat asked.

"I don't know. I didn't tell him."

They'd been on the road for about an hour when traffic suddenly started to back up.

Rosa had been squirming for the past few minutes and she suddenly realized that the pregnant woman would have to be her first consideration. And pregnant women were a subject about which she knew little. She'd sent gifts to her sisters while they were producing and to the babies when they were born—at least she'd sent her sisters money to buy gifts—but that was about as close as she'd ever come to them.

Cat glanced at her gas gauge and decided it was time to fill her tank. "I'm going to pull off the freeway at this convenience store," she said. "We're going to the reservation and I need gas. Maybe you'd like to go inside and get us some bottled water and anything else you think we should take along." Rosa simply nodded.

While Cat filled the tank, Rosa headed for the building. When she went inside to pay, Rosa was waiting at the counter with a six-pack of water, some crackers and fruit. She was pressing her hand against her lower back.

"We are going to a place that might not have such things," she said. "But if this is too much..."

"It's perfect. I never even thought of that."

The attendant took Cat's money and gave her the change. "If you're headed for the res, you might want to get off the main highway. I heard they're working a big accident that has closed off the road."

"There's another way?" Cat asked.

"Yes, ma'am. Take the road behind me until it dead-ends. Turn right and keep going about ten miles. You'll come to a small dirt road to the left. There's an old abandoned farmhouse and barn on the corner. The road don't look like much, but it'll take you about three miles in a kind of a circle and feed you right back on the interstate past the wreck."

Cat took the gravel road to where it ended, then followed the attendant's directions. But she was beginning to think she'd either misunderstood them or he hadn't told her everything. Rosa hadn't said anything, just continued to massage her lower back.

"Are you all right, Rosa?"

"I think the baby is pressing against my backbone," she said.

Thirty minutes later, Cat was ready to turn around and take her chances with the blocked road.

She didn't want to mention it, but the sky was darkening in the west. A storm was coming in. She'd already experienced a heavy Texas downpour once and that was on a paved surface. This road was dirt and gravel, and flat enough to be covered in one of those flash floods.

Suddenly the old house the attendant had mentioned came into view. Rosa seemed to buckle over and let out a mournful cry.

"What's wrong?" Cat asked.

"I am so sorry. The baby. I think it is coming now."

"No, you can't. You must stop. I'll turn around and we'll go back to San Antonio."

Cat pulled into the driveway of the house and circled around. Rosa cried again, stretched her legs out and planted her feet against the slanted floorboard.

"My water—it has broken."

"It can't be," Cat snapped. "It's in plastic bottles." She looked at Rosa's legs and felt like an idiot. "I'm sorry. I'll call an ambulance."

"No, please. I have no money."

"I do." Cat reached for her cell phone and punched in 9-1-1. No service. Damn! Here she was out the middle of nowhere with no service for her phone and no idea of where they were. What was it with emergencies and cell phones?

"Help me lie down," Rosa said between pants. "Let me get in the back."

But the back was full of ramps. "There's no room back there. Let me check out the house."

BACK ON THE FREEWAY, there was no room for either Jesse or the white truck with the primed fender to move over to the exit lane when Cat pulled off. In fact, from where the other truck was, Jesse doubted the driver even knew that Cat had left the freeway. Jesse himself wouldn't have seen her if he hadn't been in his big Dodge Ram truck. True, the driver of the white truck should be his concern—he was the criminal. But it was Cat's exit that forced him to flick on his emergency lights and make his way over.

Inch by inch he finally made it onto the shoulder and to the next exit, keeping his eyes on the boxed-in truck ahead. Not reporting his actions to headquarters was breaking a rule. Now he was putting a woman ahead of a criminal who was within reach.

Crossing the interstate and reaching the entry on-ramp took time. Finally he made it back to the convenience station and went inside.

"There were two women in here earlier," he said to

the attendant. "A blonde and a pregnant Mexican. Do you know where they went?"

"Oh, yes. I told them about a way to get around the wreck and the traffic. Good-looking blonde. Is she yours?"

"She's mine," Jesse snapped.

He took the same directions from the attendant, ran back to his truck and drove off in search of Cat. He cursed himself for letting her get away. He should have known she wasn't the kind to sit and wait. He'd have to answer to his captain for allowing the driver of the white truck to get away. At least the white truck wouldn't know she was gone until it was too late to trace her.

He hoped.

There was no sign of Cat; not even swirling road dust to say she'd come this way. Suppose he'd lost her? Elizabeth was apparently missing and now Cat had disappeared. An unwelcome chill shivered down his spine.

AGAINST her better judgment, Cat retrieved her camping equipment from her tool chest. She unfolded her sleeping bag on the old farmhouse porch and helped Rosa to it. She could tell that Rosa's pains were intense, though they didn't seem to be too close together.

"Are you sure you don't want to try to get back to

San Antonio? I feel like that young girl in *Gone With the Wind*. I don't know a thing 'bout birthing no babies."

"I've never had one before, but I've helped deliver my brothers and sisters."

"Tell me what to do." Every movie she'd ever seen dictated that a fire had to be built and water boiled. That, she could do. She pushed open the sagging door to the house and peered inside. There was a fireplace and apparently it had been used fairly recently. She didn't know if that made her feel good or not. Still, a fire would keep her occupied while she figured out their next move.

Rosa let out a moan.

"Rosa, are you okay?" Cat hurried back to the porch.

"Yes." Her reply was strained.

Oh, Jesse, I wish you were here. She might be able to handle her photography business but life was reminding her how inexperienced she was. "I'm going to build a fire in the fireplace and boil some water. Listen and call out if you hear a car coming."

Cat gathered branches and dried grass, which she arranged in the fireplace. From her camping equipment, she pulled out matches and lit the tinder. Minutes later she had a small blaze going. The chimney seemed to be drawing fine; so she could relax her fear of setting the house on fire.

Listening to her assistant's irregular breathing, she

chastised herself for coming out here, for ever offering her a job. If she'd left the woman alone, she'd be back in San Antonio with people who knew about these things.

Cat had always considered herself a kind person but she'd always traveled alone. Why she'd suddenly decided to become a Good Samaritan was beyond her. It had started with Jesse and the accident. From that moment on, her life seemed to have taken a drastic change of direction. Now she was responsible for a woman whose last name she didn't even know and a child who was about to be born. And nobody knew where they were. Why hadn't she told Jesse?

That's when she heard the sound of a car.

"Someone's coming," Cat yelled, and started toward the road, jumping and waving her arms like a cheerleader in a championship game.

The vehicle pulled in behind hers. The driver's door opened and a man got out.

"Jesse!" She ran forward and fell into his arms. "I've never been so glad to see somebody."

"I'm glad to see you, too," he growled, and hugged her tightly. "You're all right? He didn't find you?"

"He, who? I—you don't understand," she said, tearing herself away. "It's Rosa—she's having her baby." She grabbed his hand and pulled him across the dirt yard and onto the porch where Rosa was arching her back and trying to hold back a cry.

"Did you call 9-1-1?" he asked, jamming his gun under his belt at his back as he dropped down beside the woman.

"I tried, but my phone has no service here."

"Go get mine out of the truck. Maybe it will work."

It didn't.

By the time she got back, Jesse was timing Rosa's contractions.

"Law officers know about these things. You've delivered a baby, haven't you?" Cat asked.

Jesse shook his head. "No, I haven't." He thought of the weekend seminar he'd just completed. "Though I've had a little training. Where'd you get the sleeping bag?"

"I carry an assortment of supplies in my toolbox. I never know what I'll need."

Jesse let out a dry laugh.

"What's funny about that?"

"Nothing." The sex toys he'd thought she carried had turned out to be camping equipment. "The sky is getting darker and the wind is picking up. I hope the rain holds off."

"What do you do first?" Cat asked.

"*We* do first," he corrected.

"Okay, *we*."

"We need to move her inside. I can see the sky through this tin roof and we're going to need to keep her dry."

"I don't think she can get up."

Jesse reached down and picked Rosa up. "Bring the sleeping bag."

Cat gathered it and quickly spread the bag in front of the fireplace.

As Jesse laid her down, Rosa groaned and muttered something that sounded like, "Help me!"

"Do something, Jesse. Don't you have some kind of book of procedures?" Cat asked.

"Book? No. Maybe you ought to get some more firewood before it starts to rain," he told Cat. "I'll...I'll mentally review the procedure."

"Good idea."

The first drop of rain fell in front of her, hitting the dry dirt and making the dust fly. Hurriedly, she gathered two loads of branches and rotted boards, then brought in the case of bottled water.

"I don't suppose you have any towels or blankets in that tool chest? Maybe a piece of plastic?"

"I do. But the only plastic I have is a tarpaulin." By the time she retrieved them and a collapsible cooking pot that she filled with the bottled water, the rain had begun to fall in earnest. "What now?"

"We put the tarp beneath her and a blanket to cover

it." Jesse tried to recall what the instructor had said in the seminar. Not much help, since she'd said to call 9-1-1 and the dispatcher would walk them through it until an ambulance arrived at the scene.

Rosa groaned. "I believe the baby is coming."

"Cat, can you see the baby's head?"

"Not likely. That would mean I'd have to be looking."

"Well, look."

"Jesse James Dane, you're the man with the answers—you look."

Rosa lifted her skirt and leaned forward. "Please. I believe both of you had better look."

They did.

"I think we watch for the top of the baby's head," Jesse said.

"I don't see it," Cat said, a quiver in her voice.

Then Rosa cried out and lifted her pelvis off the floor.

"Oops. I think I see it now," Cat cried as the baby's head appeared.

"Clean the mucus from its nose and mouth," Jesse said, throwing Cat a towel.

At that point, Cat forgot any misgivings she had and followed Jesse's orders. He was calm and confident. She could be the same. Another push and the baby was delivered. Cat reached to catch it.

"It's slippery." She would have dropped it had Jesse not reached down with the towel and caught the squirming infant. Moments later it began to cry with great force.

Jesse cleaned the baby's face and handed it to Cat.

"Now we tie off the cord."

"With what?"

"Do you have some twine in the truck?"

"Look in the toolbox."

"Please...tell me. Is it a girl?" Rosa asked.

"I don't know," Cat admitted, "I haven't looked." She unfolded the towel and gave the baby a quick look. "It's a girl, Rosa. Who else would come into this world angry with it?" she said with a chuckle.

"She is early. Is she...all right, Ms. McCade?"

"I don't know," Cat said helplessly. She took a good look at the newborn. "She's awfully red, but she looks okay."

Jesse returned, carrying a knife and a ball of what looked like kite string. He tied the cord off and clipped it, then handed the child to her mother. "Look, Rosa. Look at your daughter."

Rosa took the bundle and held it close, pressing her lips to her daughter's cheek. "A girl. Her grandfather will not care about a girl child. We will be fine."

And they would be, Cat thought, if she had anything to do with it. She sat by the fireplace and tested the water. It certainly wasn't boiling but it was warm. With the towel, she moved the cooking pot to the hearth.

"Let me clean her." Cat took the child, laid her across her lap, and moistened the corner of a towel. As she washed the baby's face, the little girl seemed to focus her eyes on Cat. There was no fear. Her expression was one of wonder and acceptance.

Cat felt a great warm swell of tenderness. This was a special moment, a spiritual connection between herself and this tiny human being. Just for a second, she wondered what it would be like to have her own child. Jesse's child. The baby caught Cat's finger and held it.

When she was finally done cleaning the infant, she found Rosa covered with the zippered top of the sleeping bag, her eyes closed. Cat handed the baby to Jesse. "Hold her while I tidy up," she whispered, her throat tight with emotion.

She gathered the soiled towels and blanket and carried them to the truck. The rain had slowed to a gentle patter on the tin roof. When she returned, Rosa was sleeping and Jesse was sitting on the floor, leaning against the wall by the fireplace. He was holding the baby they'd delivered, his chin resting on the child's head. As she watched, he stopped moving and closed his eyes. Both he and the baby were asleep. The glow of the fire gave his stern face a softness that made Cat's heart swell.

Rosa and her baby needed to get to the hospital, but something made Cat delay leaving this place and this moment.

Delivering Rosa's baby had been an incredible experience. Bringing new life into the world made everything seem good. She'd never held a newborn, yet the moment Jesse put Rosa's child in her arms, she'd felt such an overwhelming rush that she couldn't explain it, even to herself. Her heart raced. Her breath came short and fast. But the crowning moment was when the baby had opened her eyes and looked at Cat. They'd connected and she understood the phrase "time stood still." She wished she could capture this moment on film.

That's just what she'd do. She stood, slipped out of the house and dashed to her El Camino to retrieve her best camera.

Quietly reentering the farmhouse, she adjusted the settings and began to snap photographs of Jesse and the child. What she was capturing would never go on a calendar or a catalog. These photographs were hers.

Jesse and a baby.

She was capturing innocence, trust, faith—that one moment where nothing was spoiled, where problems were out there beyond their little haven. She sniffed and swallowed hard. For now, life was good.

11

JESSE IN HIS TRUCK, with Cat following in hers, took Rosa and her baby to the nearest hospital emergency room. The hospital staff had been alerted as soon as Jesse found a service zone for his cell phone and a nurse team met Jesse's truck at the door and moved Rosa to a gurney. The baby was whisked to the neonatal unit as they tried to maneuver Rosa through the frantic group of people crowded around an incoming ambulance.

The accident victim was unloaded and wheeled into the trauma unit. Cat couldn't see the victim but she could tell from the frantic pace of the nurses and the blood on the sheet that it was serious.

Cat figured that Rosa would be admitted for the night but Cat had no intention of leaving the hospital before she knew that Rosa and the baby were okay. Jesse took charge and found a seat for Cat, then went to a quiet spot to call Szachon. He was soon back. He slid his arm around Cat as if it were the most natural thing in the world. She snuggled against him, seeking the comfort that he offered.

"Szachon wasn't there. Elizabeth called and he went to meet her."

"Is she all right?"

"Austin didn't know. He said that Szachon left in a hurry to go wherever she is. I explained that we're at the hospital and Austin said he'll tell Szachon when he gets back."

Jesse and Cat sat in the waiting room and watched the other people. Some were holding hands. Some were crying. Some were laughing as if whatever brought them to this place of hurt and pain was nothing serious. "I guess you're probably accustomed to emergency rooms," Cat said.

"As a state trooper, I saw too much of this kind of suffering. That's why I applied to ranger school. Hunting bad guys and solving crimes is easier. The truth is, you never get accustomed to this," Jesse said. "You just have to learn that it's part of your job. People depend on you and you do your best. When everything works out, it's good. When it doesn't, you...well, you just go on."

Cat sighed. "I read somewhere that people in law enforcement have a lot of marital problems. I can see why that would happen."

"True. I have friends who couldn't do without their wives' support. The lucky ones swear that having someone to share it with keeps them sane. Others can't take the pressure and split up. It's tough."

"What do you do to get through it?" Cat asked, leaning forward and looking into his dark face.

"I get on my bike and ride and ride until my mind is clear. Then I come home, shower and put on my uniform and go to work. What do you do?"

"The same thing. How can two people so different be so much alike?"

"Maybe," he said slowly, thoughtfully, "we're both trying to escape the needs of our parents. Your father sent you down a path where you never stayed in one spot long enough to take root. And my mother needed someone to cling to. I always thought my brothers cut me off from my mother. I think now that it was her pain that sent me running.

"And," he continued, "we both reacted in the same way. You take care of underprivileged people, like Rosa. And I became a ranger."

He was right. Why hadn't she seen it?

"So, what are we going to do?"

"Until we find out what Szachon is going to do about SterlingWear, I don't know," Cat said.

"Well, I'm still a Texas Ranger, that is if I can figure out what I'm going to do about you."

She caught her breath. "Do I need to have something done about me?"

"I don't have a clue what *you* need, Cat, or even if

you need anything. It's my need that's driving me crazy."

The waiting room seemed to go silent as Cat's gaze melded with Jesse's. "What kind of need?" she whispered.

"I need—"

"Jesse! Cat! Have you seen her? How is she?"

Sterling Szachon came tearing through the waiting area to where they were sitting. He was followed by Vadin and a hotel security guard.

Cat swallowed hard and pulled away from Jesse's embrace. "She's fine. The baby is a girl."

Szachon looked confused. "What baby?"

"Rosa's. We delivered her baby in an old abandoned house," Cat answered, equally confused.

Szachon shook his head. "But what about Elizabeth? The police called. She was in a wreck on the freeway and they brought her here."

"Is she hurt?" Cat asked.

"Yes, but I don't know how badly."

"Wreck?" Jesse stood. "Did they say what she was driving?"

"That's the thing of it," Szachon said. "She wasn't driving. She was a passenger in a white truck. The driver took off and just left her. Who would do a thing like that?"

"So Elizabeth was responsible for the threats?" Szachon shook his head in disbelief.

"It seems so—with help from the driver, one of your disgruntled hotel employees who needed money," Jesse explained, "and had access to the hotel."

"But why? I don't understand."

The hospital had made one of the small conference rooms available for Szachon's use while Elizabeth was in surgery to repair a broken arm and a deep laceration in her hip. Her prognosis was good.

"It's all my fault," Vadin said. "She needed me and I wasn't there for her." He leaned forward, his face in his hands. "I was a fool. I can't lose her now."

"But why?" Cat asked. "Why go through all this? If she didn't want to run SterlingWear, why not say so?"

Szachon paced back and forth. "I didn't give her a chance. When she called me, she was distraught. I caught the next plane, packed her things and brought her back. I'm not sure she expected that."

"I would have done the same thing," Jesse said. "If a man thinks a woman he cares about is in danger, he'll protect her, no matter what."

He looked at Cat, remembering his decision to follow her instead of the truck. If he'd intercepted the white truck, he would have stopped an accident and exposed the stalker. Instead he'd followed Cat.

"Vadin," Szachon said, "I don't know what Elizabeth wants, but if you care about her, I think the two of you had better do some serious talking. I don't know why she did what she did, but she must have been desperate."

Raoul took in a deep breath, stood and shook Szachon's hand. "Whatever Elizabeth wants is what she'll get. I promise I'll never put her through anything like this again."

LATER THAT EVENING Cat and Jesse were allowed to see Rosa who was going to be kept overnight as a precaution. Just as they were about to leave, Pappy came in, beaming from ear to ear.

"How'd you know?" Cat asked.

"Rosa, she told the nurse to call me. I thank you, Ms. McCade, for bringing this child into the world. And you, too, Ranger Dane. And don't worry. If you need any more men to wear the underwear, all you have to do is say the word and you'll have them."

On their way back to Szachon's private conference room, they went by the nursery where the attendant brought the baby to the glass for them to see. As if she knew who was watching, she put her arm to her mouth, then held it up and pursed her lips as if she were throwing them a kiss.

Cat gasped and reached for Jesse's hand without knowing she'd done so. Jesse threaded his fingers through hers. He knew Cat had no wish to have children, but she was obviously as touched as he. He was seeing a warm spot in her heart, first for Rosa, now for Rosa's child.

"I hope she grows up to be as special as she is now," Jesse finally said, "but a single mother with no education, I don't know."

"Then we'll have to help her," Cat announced. "We saved her life—now we're responsible for it. All she needs is a decent job and a place to live. Oh, Jesse, we'll have to do something to help her find both. We can be Aunt Cat and Uncle Jesse."

Jesse liked the sound of the "we." But he'd seen too many of these situations to have the simple faith that Cat did. He hated to burst her bubble but it was better that she didn't get too carried away. "Aunt Cat," he said. "Sure we can, if you stick around. Seems to me that you are already Aunt Cat to your sisters' children. How often do you see them?"

"Well, not often, but they don't need me."

He stopped and turned Cat so that her back was to the wall of the empty corridor where they were walking. He continued to hold her one hand but put his other hand on the wall beside her, boxing her in. "How do you know?"

"Well, I don't. But they have parents and grandparents...and I'm gone so much." She frowned. "Maybe they do, but I've never thought they did. Why are you trying to make me feel bad, Jesse?"

"Because you said in the beginning that one of your personal rules is that your relationships are temporary. Remember?" He tossed out the words, hoping she'd contradict them. "How will that apply when it comes to Rosa and her baby?"

"Rules! Is that all you can think about? I'll admit that I've been a failure with my nieces and nephews, but this is different. You don't have to get involved or even agree, but I can help Rosa and she needs me."

"And what do *you* need, Cat?"

His words jarred her. Cat stared at him, helplessly. What did she need? "My freedom. My work."

"And what are you prepared to give in return for your needs being met?" he asked.

"I don't know," she whispered.

"Well, when you find out, then we'll talk about needs." He let his arms fall limply to his sides and walked away.

"Where are you going, Jesse?"

"I'm going to send the security guard to drive you back to the hotel in your truck. Szachon and I will stay there until we find out what happened." He turned and left her. He had to do that before he ended up kissing her.

Cat stood, watching him disappear into the conference room. Moments later, the guard appeared and waited for her to accompany him to her truck.

Woodenly, she followed him. She had no reason to join the Szachons. She wasn't family. They weren't even friends. Pappy was with Rosa and Jesse was gone. This time he really was gone. And she hadn't stopped him.

He was right. She'd always discouraged anyone from becoming too close, letting them into her life for only a temporary moment. "Look, but don't touch" had become her motto.

Now she was alone.

JESSE HAD NEVER FELT such emptiness. He and Cat had shared something that he'd never forget, but it was only temporary. She was caught up in the moment with Rosa and the baby, and wanted to absorb the goodness of that moment. But it wouldn't last. If SterlingWear was canceled, she'd be on to her next assignment, still proving to her father that she could be a woman in her own right, without a man. If the clothing line continued...well, he didn't know. A transfer from San Antonio might be a good idea.

After the hotel security guard left to escort Cat back to the hotel, Szachon motioned for Jesse to have a seat. "We have spoken to the doctor. Elizabeth is in intensive care. Vadin is with her. It seems my little sister *was* a very desperate woman when she called me."

"Desperate about what?" Jesse asked.

"Vadin says it's all his fault. He didn't want her to work. None of the women in his family have had a career. He kept telling her she didn't have the talent to be a designer. The truth is, he knew she did and he was afraid she'd leave him."

"She cried on your shoulder and you rushed to the rescue," Jesse said, nodding. "Been there, done that. Didn't work for me, either."

Szachon stood and walked to the window. "She just wanted to shake Vadin up. Vadin couldn't believe she'd left. When I gave her a business to run, she panicked. Elizabeth expected him to come after her. But he didn't. That's when she came up with the threats. If he really cared about her, he'd come to get her."

"Well, he did. So what's going to happen now?"

Szachon shook his head. "I don't know. It's up to Elizabeth. We are going forward with SterlingWear. Daisy can run it if Elizabeth doesn't want to. And, of course, Cat will still handle the catalog work."

"You think Cat will stay?"

"Of course she will. We have a contract. Besides, I'm beginning to think that there's something else that will keep her here."

"What?" Jesse asked, not certain he wanted to know.

"You," Szachon said.

"You're wrong," Jesse protested. "She doesn't need a husband. And I don't believe in significant others."

Szachon shrugged and smiled. "I can't argue with that. I'm not ready for that kind of thing myself."

Yes, you are, Jesse thought. If Szachon didn't want a wife, Jesse knew just the person to change his mind. Bettina.

FOR THE NEXT MONTH Cat photographed hundreds of potential models. A great many more than she'd ever intended, but when she'd found out that every prospect Pappy sent had pledged a portion of his fee to a fund for Rosa's baby, Cat couldn't say no.

Though she still occupied a room in the Palace, Cat had moved her office into the Daisy's Designs building. Szachon's former significant other had proved to be a helpful ally. From Szachon she'd learned that Jesse was out of the doghouse with his captain and the city of San Antonio officials. He was currently involved in a ten-year-old unsolved murder of a child. His life was back to normal. She guessed that's what he needed.

Rosa had found temporary work as a nanny for a child the same age as her baby. The woman traveled and was happy to have Rose live in and take care of both children. That situation made Cat uncomfortable for it wasn't quite the scenario she'd envisioned for her goddaughter.

As the purse from Pappy's prospects grew, an idea began to form at the back of Cat's mind. What about a house for other women like Rosa? Cat took the idea to Szachon, who took the ball and ran with it. They'd decided to introduce SterlingWear with a big, expensive, charity ball. The money raised would be the start of a fund for Rosa's House.

In the meantime, a happy Elizabeth returned to London to set up the European branch of SterlingWear. She'd run the business with the help of her husband. With Daisy's input, Cat had made the final selections for their catalog models and started shooting.

Weeks passed without any word from Jesse. Every time Cat left the hotel, she looked up and down the street. She never saw a single man who looked like Jesse. A hundred times she picked up the phone to call him to tell him—what? That she missed him? That she wanted to talk about her work with him? That she wanted to hear what he was doing in his search for the little girl?

For the first time there was a sense of incompleteness to her life. The catalog mockup was complete—except for the cover, for which she couldn't settle on any of the photographs in her portfolio.

From her hotel window Cat watched as people

walked along the River Walk, hand in hand, arm and arm. It was late. She hadn't been able to sleep. No matter how much she tried, she couldn't stop thinking about Jesse. About him delivering Rosa's baby. About restaurant owner Estelle's fondness for a man who'd found her wayward son and brought him home. About Jesse's dedication to his work. About his body and how it made her burn.

But this was what they both wanted, wasn't it? A temporary relationship where he went home and she moved on? That was what she'd always wanted out of her relationships. But now all she wanted was Jesse.

IT WAS ALMOST MIDNIGHT when Jesse knocked on Cat's hotel room door.

When he'd started out two hours ago, he'd headed for the open highway and had ended up at the house where Rosa's baby had been born. He'd signed on for a case that had taken him out of San Antonio. But that hadn't stopped him from coming back to see Cat.

She opened the door. "Jesse." She blinked, then said, "Is there something wrong?"

"Yes, there's something wrong. May I come in?"

"Of course." She turned and went back inside.

That's when he saw that she was wearing the flannel shirt. His shirt. "I didn't know if you'd still be in the hotel. It seems that you turned out not to be so temporary."

"I still haven't decided about that," she said. "Once I settle on a model for the SterlingWear catalog cover, I will have fulfilled my contract."

"So, you're leaving?"

"I don't know. Szachon has offered me a permanent job with SterlingWear. Did you get your bike repaired?"

"I did."

"Did you bring the bill?"

"No." He dropped his hat on the couch and took a step closer.

She stepped back. "Doesn't matter. Let me get my purse—I'll write you a check." She went into her bedroom.

Jesse followed, drawn by a force he couldn't shake off.

"Forget the bill, Cat," Jesse said, closing the door behind him. He gestured toward her with his hand. "Why are you wearing my shirt?"

"Because it's...soft." Her voice was a throaty whisper. "If you want it, I'll return it."

"No." The lamp beside the bed cast a glow across the sheet, which was rumpled from where she'd lain. The silk spread was twisted, one corner of it totally dislodged. "No," he repeated more firmly. He balled his fists. He shouldn't have started this. He should go and never touch her again.

"Jesse? What's wrong?"

With a groan, he reached out and suddenly she was in his arms. His mouth found hers and her lips went wild with passion. He stripped the buttons from the shirt as he tore it from her body. She arched against him, nude except for a wisp of lace panties.

Then, just as suddenly as it had started, Jesse forced himself to stop. He let Cat go and stood, breathing deeply for a long minute before he said, "If you want me to go, say so."

"I don't want you to go."

"If I make love to you, that's what it will be, Cat, making love. So think about this and make sure."

She raised her eyes, planting her gaze on his face. "I'm sure."

"I'm breaking my own rule coming here," he said, "and I don't plan to leave."

"I'm not going to let you go," she said, and reached for the buttons on his shirt. He pushed her hands away, lifted her and laid her on the bed. He sat on the bed and tugged off his boots, leaned back and removed his shirt. Then he stood and let his trousers fall to the floor.

"Jesse!" Cat exclaimed with a laugh. "You're wearing a SterlingWear thong."

"I absolutely am," he said, falling on top of her. He smiled and stroked her hair. "Any good husband supports his wife's business."

"Husband?"

They simply looked at each other, drinking in his words and what they meant. He knew he was being intense and he struggled to soften that fierceness.

"If you'll have me. If not, we'll live together for as long as you're here. I won't try to stop you from going."

"You'd better," she said. "Just so you know it, your house isn't big enough for us, but I certainly don't intend to have a picket fence in the suburbs, either."

"You won't have to. I've already bought us a place." He kissed her, softly, gently, over and over again as he spoke. "I bought the old farmhouse where Rosa's baby was born. You interested in helping me restore it?"

She slid her arms around his neck and shifted her body seductively beneath him. "I'm interested. But you do realize it's falling down."

"Then it's going to take us a long time."

"Mmm-hmm."

He left her lips and moved down, following the lines of her neck to her breast. "Cat?"

"Yes, Jesse."

"Your SterlingWear is going to be a big success. Lots of repeat buying."

"Why?"

"Because this flimsy little thong is never going to survive a good tumble in the bedroom."

She laughed and pushed him up and onto his back. "Sure it will. If your woman takes it off." She straddled him, giving him a wicked smile as she teased the hard mound beneath the thong with her fingertips. Hooking her thumbs underneath the edges of the garment, she ran her fingers beneath the fabric until he was nearly wild. Then she tugged gently. And tugged again.

"We may have to test the product durability right here and now. I think the problem is that you need a larger size." She finally admitted, "I can't get it off."

"I can," he said and, with a growl, he ripped the strap and slung the thong against the wall. Then he turned back to Cat, more serious now. "I'll leave this up to you, Cat. You're the woman I want to spend the rest of my life with, the woman I love."

"Love?"

"Yes. I wasn't looking for this, but it's happened."

"Not yet, it hasn't," she suddenly teased, and moved aside, lying on her back. She reached for him. "Make love to me, Jesse—now and tomorrow and the day after. Hold me close—I don't ever want to be alone again."

He moved over her, entering her slowly and powerfully. "Tell me you love me."

"I love you, Jesse James Dane."

He could feel her trembling response, tightening and loosening. She *loved* him. Then he forgot any thought he had of moving slowly and knew that she was with him with every thrust. Making love to Cat was more than a physical joining, it was a merger of the soul for both.

CAT SLIPPED OUT OF BED and opened the drapes. The sun was rising, curling butterfly wings of soft yellow over the eastern landscape. Then Jesse was behind her. He put his arms around her and rested his chin on her shoulder.

"Sunrise," he said, giving her a kiss. "And I'm seeing it with you."

"You said you never stayed until morning."

"Until now."

"Jesse, let me photograph you. I've never photographed anyone I loved before."

He couldn't deny her. "And I've never been photographed by the woman I loved."

He headed for the bedroom, looking around. He rescued the damaged thong and shook his head. "Looks like this is worthless."

"Never fear. You're dealing with a woman who is prepared." She pulled a bag out of the closet and dumped an assortment of SterlingWear products onto the bed. "Choose one."

"Any boxers?"

She pulled out her camera and checked the settings. "None. This one is perfect for you," she said, grabbing up a pair. "It's called 'Outlaw.'"

She flung a skimpy pair of black bikini underwear at him.

"Think they'll fit?" he asked.

"Well," Cat said with a smile playing across her lips, "not unless you hurry."

It was a tight fit, but he got them on, then reached for his trousers.

"Oh, no. SterlingWear men don't wear pants."

"I already told you, I'm not one of your models. Maybe this isn't such a good idea."

Cat loved that he was willing to do something that so obviously made him feel awkward. She gave him a quick kiss. "Come stand by the mirror. I want all of you in this shot."

From there he moved to the bedroom, where she lured him back into bed with promises and kisses. As she snapped the camera, she continued to touch him. "Is this how you get your models to do what you want?" he said, eyebrows raised.

"Only the one I want to make love to me," she said, and put her camera away.

An hour later and Cat's loudly protesting stomach forced them to dress and call for room service.

"So," Cat said hesitantly, "when did you know that you loved me?"

"I think it was the same time you knew—when we delivered Rosa's baby."

She nodded. "Yes. I think I knew before that, but when you went to sleep holding the child, my heart just melted." Then her eyes lit up like a little girl's. "So, when do we get married?"

"Tomorrow," was Jesse's prompt reply.

Her mouth dropped open. "No. I have to buy a dress and—well, do you think we could hold our service in that little church beside your house? Oh, and I have to call my family—and hand me the phone. I have to call my maid of honor."

"Your maid of honor?"

She held up her hand for him to wait and punched in the number. "Hello, Bettina. Guess what?"

Epilogue

CAT STEPPED into the red dress she'd bought the first night she arrived, and glanced in the mirror, remembering Jesse unzipping it for her. She'd never get used to the short skirt and the high heels Daisy had insisted she buy.

"Perfect for Zon's big party," Daisy had said earlier. "You're the one responsible for the SterlingWear catalog and the exhibit. You have to look like a star in front of these guests. After all, half the money in Texas has been spent on tickets to the dinner-dance."

Cat was forced to agree. She reached behind her and caught the tab on the zipper and pulled. It ran along smoothly for a moment, then caught. "Damn! Stuck again. Jesse!" she called.

"Yes?" He stepped into the doorway, his attention on the studs he was fastening in his shirt. Tonight he'd swapped his ranger uniform for a black tux. Behind him the lights of their first Christmas tree blinked in splashes of red and green. No fancy, trendy tree for the all-American boy; he wanted a regular Christmas. Then he raised his gaze to her and let out a whistle.

"This zipper's stuck again," she said. "What if it won't work? I have nothing else to wear." She started to let the dress slide down.

"Don't worry—I'll zip you up. This is going to be the beginning of something big and you can't miss it. Just think of all that ticket money Zon is donating to the women's shelter you and Rosa set up."

"Yes, but it's still not enough."

"Most of your underwear models have donated their pay, haven't they?" Jesse said, zipping the dress and clasping his arms around her.

"I know, and we're very grateful. But I'm worried about SterlingWear. Daisy and I still haven't decided on the cover and that's the key image. You have to grab the buyer at first glance."

"That's what you keep saying." Jesse pushed Cat toward the front door, stopping briefly to don his string tie and slip his arms into his jacket. "Out of all those photographs, surely you found one that would work."

"Yes, but he's shy. He doesn't want to be a cover model."

Jesse tied his Texas string tie and held out his arm. "If anybody can change his mind, it's you. Shall we?"

"Just a minute, I want to get my camera," Cat said.

"Not tonight. Tonight you're my lady. Let somebody else take the photographs."

No Hollywood premier could have been more elaborate. The River Walk was closed to everyone but guests of Sterling Szachon. A red-jacketed valet took the Ram truck and disappeared, leaving Jesse and Cat to walk down the red carpet with the other guests. The ballroom was lined with eight-foot-tall shadow boxes draped in red velvet. In the middle were tables covered with candle-filled globes.

"This is really something," Jesse said. "What's behind the curtains?"

"A photograph of the pages in our catalog. Where are we sitting?"

"Over here, girlfriend," Daisy called. "We're right up front."

Their table included Daisy, Bull, Rosa, Pappy and Father Mulvaney.

The meal was exquisite, the music beautiful. Finally, after the dessert was served, Sterling Szachon stepped up behind the microphone.

"Good evening, friends. Welcome. Tonight we introduce SterlingWear, our new line of men's undergarments. In addition to the funds derived from your generous donations, ten percent of every purchase will be donated to Rosa's House, our center for women."

There was an outbreak of applause.

At that moment a waiter came and whispered in Daisy's ear. She stood. "Cat, will you excuse us, please? We made a little change in the plans. I hope you'll like it. Pappy, Father, will you two and Jesse give me a hand?''

"I'll come, too," Cat said.

Jesse leaned over and whispered in her ear. "No, please sit here. I have a gift for you, and I think when you see it, you'll understand."

The four conspirators cut behind the curtains and the lights went down.

"When you leave," Zon went on, "there will be catalogs for everyone, the same catalogs that go into the mail next week to introduce our products. But you're about to get a headstart. My father always read the newspaper beginning with the back page. So we're going to do the same."

A spotlight covered the first box.

"This is page twelve of the catalog." The red cover fell from the box to reveal a Santa wearing a fur thong and a Santa Hat, standing beside a Christmas tree and holding a flute of champagne. Applause broke out and the Santa lifted his glass and stepped out of the frame. The photograph had come to life.

That was a wonderful idea. Real models instead of the photographs. Cat clapped enthusiastically.

"Page eleven."

One by one the pages were revealed and Cat

watched the men she'd coaxed into just the right look come to life.

She'd done it. Her photographs were going to work. She was happy that she'd accepted Szachon's offer to handle the photography and design for all his company catalogs and advertising media. Daisy would handle manufacturing and someone else had been hired to handle sales and accounting.

She and Jesse hadn't set a date for the wedding yet. It wasn't Jesse's idea. It was Cat. She wasn't quite ready. It was just too hard to believe that her life was changing so dramatically and that she could trust the dream she was following.

Daisy came back to sit beside Cat in the darkness. "I hope you don't mind that we decided to feature the live models instead of using their photographs. Zon thought that since these men had donated their fees to Rosa's House, they should be honored.

"I'm stunned. But what about the cover? I never decided. None of the photographs seemed right."

"Well, I think you're going to like it. As a matter of fact, it was the model's idea."

Page nine brought the house down when Pappy, wearing a tank top, boxers and a tool belt, turned and gave the audience a grin.

But nothing prepared the onlookers for Bull, wearing an abbreviated harem jacket, briefs and pixie shoes.

At last, they were down to the last box, the box nearest to Cat's table. Cat frowned, thinking hard. They'd waffled back and forth, nobody really confident about a choice for the cover.

"For the final box, the Sterling Man. Not a professional model, but a man of duty, a man who spends his life making the world safe. A man every woman wants to take home and keep. The model for the photograph chosen to be on the cover is a man who would never have agreed to do this were it not for the lady in his life.

"A drumroll, please. May I present the cover of the SterlingWear catalog."

The red curtain fell and Cat gasped.

Jesse.

The photograph was the one she'd made of him the morning they'd watched the sun rise. He was standing in front of the mirror. The mirror caught the reflection of her looking at him just before she'd snapped the shot. Both then and now, she was looking at him with eyes filled with love.

He stepped out of the frame and down beside her, then held out his hand. "What do you think, am I the Sterling Man?"

"Oh, yes." She shook her head with wonder. "I can't believe you did this," she said. "You swore you'd never pose for my catalog."

"Since I've met you, I've really become an outlaw,

just like my namesake. You've made me break all the rules—even my own. I love you, Catherine McCade. Let's get married."

She put her arms around his neck and pulled his face down to meet hers. "I love you, too. And you're definitely going to marry me."

Jesse shook his head. "Still giving me orders."

"That I am. Put on your clothes, Ranger. These women have looked long enough. And I'm the only one who's going to touch."

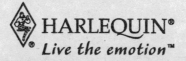

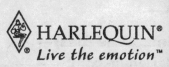

If you enjoyed what you just read,
then we've got an offer you can't resist!

Take 2 bestselling
love stories FREE!

Plus get a FREE surprise gift!

Clip this page and mail it to Harlequin Reader Service®

IN U.S.A.	IN CANADA
3010 Walden Ave.	P.O. Box 609
P.O. Box 1867	Fort Erie, Ontario
Buffalo, N.Y. 14240-1867	L2A 5X3

YES! Please send me 2 free Harlequin Temptation® novels and my free surprise gift. After receiving them, if I don't wish to receive anymore, I can return the shipping statement marked cancel. If I don't cancel, I will receive 4 brand-new novels each month, before they're available in stores. In the U.S.A., bill me at the bargain price of $3.57 plus 25¢ shipping and handling per book and applicable sales tax, if any*. In Canada, bill me at the bargain price of $4.24 plus 25¢ shipping and handling per book and applicable taxes**. That's the complete price and a savings of 10% off the cover prices—what a great deal! I understand that accepting the 2 free books and gift places me under no obligation ever to buy any books. I can always return a shipment and cancel at any time. Even if I never buy another book from Harlequin, the 2 free books and gift are mine to keep forever.

142 HDN DNT5
342 HDN DNT6

Name	(PLEASE PRINT)	
Address	Apt.#	
City	State/Prov.	Zip/Postal Code

 * Terms and prices subject to change without notice. Sales tax applicable in N.Y.
** Canadian residents will be charged applicable provincial taxes and GST.
   All orders subject to approval. Offer limited to one per household and not valid to
   current Harlequin Temptation® subscribers.
   ® are registered trademarks of Harlequin Enterprises Limited.

TEMP02   ©1998 Harlequin Enterprises Limited

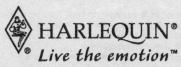

 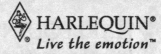

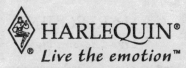